STORM AND PROMISE

SHADOW OF WHITE
BOOK 1

Blake J Soder

The characters and events portrayed in this book are fictitious. Any similarity to real persons, living or dead, is coincidental and not intended by the author.

JUNE 24

The little store sat alone on the side of the highway, miles from the nearest city – a convenient stop for anyone who forgot to fill up their tank at the last town or someone just needing directions while on their way either to or from Grand Rapids or Minneapolis.

Erik needed neither gas nor directions, but he did need food and water.

Using the side of his fist, he rubbed a clean spot in the glass of the door and peered inside. He could see shelves and wire racks near the front but it was too dark to see all the way to the back. Nevertheless, what he could see eased his worry that the store may have gone out of business and been abandoned years ago. The shelves were fully stocked.

He took a step back and tugged on the handle. The door was locked. No surprise there. The storm came at two in the morning on a Sunday. He would have been surprised if it wasn't locked.

Sliding his backpack off his shoulders, he pulled the heavy iron prybar from its loop on the side and turned to Seth.

"Okay, kiddo. You need to take a couple steps back."

Seth obeyed, taking two slow, deliberate steps backwards.

"A little more. And cover your eyes. You don't want to get glass in them."

The boy took another two steps back and covered his eyes with both hands. He was small and slightly built, with blue eyes, straight blonde hair, and several days' worth of dirt on his face, neck, and arms. He looked even smaller in his baggy jeans and dirty, over-sized t-shirt. Erik guessed he was around ten years old, not more than twelve. He couldn't be sure because Seth hadn't spoken a word since he'd found him sitting on the front steps of a house in Hill City last week.

Gauging Seth was safely out of the way, Erik turned back to the door. It was a single pane of thick, tempered glass in a steel frame. He stepped off to the side before drawing back with the iron bar and swinging it into the glass.

The kickback from the bar stung his palms and set his hands to tingling but did little more than make a small bullseye of cracks in the glass.

Shaking one hand at a time and flexing his fingers, he glanced back to Seth, making sure the boy was still standing back and covering his eyes.

He adjusted his grip on the bar and took a breath before drawing back again. This time, he stepped into the swing. The glass door exploded, showering him and the whole front of the store with thousands of small, sharp squares.

After brushing the glass from his hair and shoulders, he used the flat end of the bar to clear the rest from the edges of the steel frame. He turned back to Seth. The boy was still standing patiently with his hands over his eyes. A few of the glass squares had landed in the gravel at his feet and on his sneakers.

"Okay, kiddo. You're safe."

Seth uncovered his eyes but stayed where he was.

Erik slid the bar back into the loop on the side of his backpack and then slung the pack over his shoulder. At fifteen years old, he was a little tall for his age, with broad shoulders, longish brown hair that needed cut, and hazel eyes. Like Seth, he was wearing tattered blue jeans, a dirty t-shirt, and thread-bare sneakers that had seen many more miles than they were designed for.

"You want to come in?" he asked Seth.

Not moving from where he stood, Seth cocked his head a bit and peered past Erik to the murky interior of Ed's Gas & Grocery. Shifting his gaze back to Erik, he gave a single, quick shake of his head.

"I don't think anyone's in there," Erik reassured him. He spread his arms, taking in the parking lot. "The lot's empty and the door was locked."

Seth stared at him as though he wasn't even speaking.

"Suit yourself then. Any requests?"

The boy's expression remained passive.

Erik sighed. "I'll get you some juice. How about that? Grape? Orange? Apple?"

Seth's appeared to consider the offer. After two or three seconds, he gave a single nod.

"Okay then."

He was glad he'd at least gotten some sort of reaction. He'd been afraid Seth had gone catatonic again.

"Why don't you wait by those pumps over there?" He nodded to the gas pumps on the concrete island in the middle of the small lot.

As he watched the boy shuffle across the crushed gravel to the island, he wondered if Seth would ever snap out of whatever state he was in. He didn't think Seth was mute. Even at his age, he should have learned to communicate in some way, whether through hand signals, writing, or whatever. But Seth's communication was limited solely to nods or shakes of his head, and that was only recently. When Erik first came across him, he was little more than a zombie, not responding or communicating in any way at all. The only way Erik got him to follow when he left Hill City was by taking him by the hand and leading him.

Progress is progress, Erik thought, *no matter how small,* and then smiled to himself. He was paraphrasing a line from *Horton Hears a Who,* one of his sister's favorite bedtime stories.

Turning back to the shattered door, he stepped inside and took a quick survey of the layout. Besides the sole checkout counter in the front and a couple of wire display racks, there were three isles running down the length of a single room, shelves along both walls, and a large built-in cooler in the back. A ceiling fan hung over the middle of the room, motionless now for lack of power.

Moving down the first aisle, he began filling his backpack with beef jerky, cheese sticks, nuts, dried fruit, and cereal bars. He added a handful of salted nut rolls and a couple of chocolate bars but avoided the potato chips, pastries, and anything else of little nutritional value. Crap like that would only add needless bulk to his pack. They needed survival food, not junk food.

Rounding the end of the aisle, he nearly stumbled over the corpse on the floor.

"Jesus!"

His backpack slipped from his hand as he took a quick step back.

It was a woman. She was lying on her back at the end of the second aisle, her legs bent under her. One arm lay over her stomach while the other stretched out above her head. Her long, yellow-blonde hair was splayed out around her head on the tile floor like a fiery halo. She was wearing a blue smock over her black slacks and a white short-sleeve blouse. A black nametag with white lettering was pinned to her smock above her left breast. It read EMILY.

Like everyone else who had been on their feet during the storm, Emily was dead before she even hit the floor.

Erik took a deep breath and composed himself, glancing around and assuring himself there were no other corpses hiding behind the aisles before glancing back down to the body.

Emily. It sounded like a younger woman's name but her age was hard to guess. Like all of the other bodies he'd come across, she looked as though she died a hundred years ago in some far-off desert, her body desiccated by the sun, dry winds, and sand. Her leathery skin was a dark, mottled brown and pulled tight over her bones and joints. The muscles beneath were thin and withered. Her lips were pulled back, giving her a ghoulish death grin, and her eyes were now two shriveled, pale-yellow, dead things sunken deep into their dark, hollow sockets.

He noted a gold ring with a small diamond on the third finger of her left hand. He wasn't sure if it was an engagement ring or a wedding ring, not that it mattered anymore.

Erik wondered why she had been working in a nowhere convenience store at two in the morning on a Sunday. There were no cars in the parking lot outside. Had someone – her husband or fiancé maybe – dropped her off here, intending to pick her up again later? He thought about it and then decided that knowing the answer would not make Emily any less dead. There were a lot of corpses out there now. And while most had died in their beds, he was sure he would come across at least a few more in unexpected places.

He picked up his pack, slung it back over his shoulder, and stepped carefully around the mummified corpse formerly known as Emily.

Making his way to the big cooler, he chose two plastic bottles of water and two of apple juice. They were warm. There had been no electricity since the storm and he doubted it would be coming back on any time soon. He stuffed the bottles into his backpack, thought about it, and then added two more of water. It added weight but he wasn't taking any chances. The water supply in the last town had been dry and there were no guarantees about the next.

Returning to the front of the store, he stopped at one of the display racks. It held squirt guns, playing cards, and an array of small toys. He considered the toys and then selected a small metal car about an inch long: a cobalt-blue Corvette Stingray. It looked like just the thing to keep Seth occupied while he cleared houses or scavenged through other stores along the road for supplies. Slipping the toy into his pocket, he ducked back through the door, his feet crunching on the shattered glass.

He paused to let his eyes adjust from the deep gloom inside to the lighter gloom outside. The air was still and stale, without even the hint of a breeze. A heavy, gray haze hung low in the sky like a dirty glass dome over the whole world. It had been this way for two weeks, since the morning after the storm. Weather no longer existed. Days where now shrouded in a still, grainy twilight while nights fell quickly to cold, absolute darkness.

Seth was still sitting on the edge of the concrete island in the middle of the parking lot, his back to one of the gas pumps. He was using a long, crooked stick to scratch random squiggles and lines in the dirt at his feet.

Erik walked over to the boy and mussed his hair.

"Hey, kiddo. You ready to hit the road again?"

Seth glanced up, smiled, and gave a quick nod. He dropped his stick and got to his feet.

Erik looked up at the hazy sky. He took a deep breath and then blew it out.

"I figure we've got another couple of hours before dark. Aitkin is just a few miles down the road." He glanced back down to Seth. "Think we can make it?"

Seth copied him, glancing up at the sky and appearing to give it some serious study before looking back to Erik. He gave a short, affirmative nod.

"Good enough, dude," Erik said, grinning and mussing the boy's hair again.

He did not want to get caught on the road again when darkness fell. That had happened his first night after leaving Grand Rapids, about a week before he came across Seth. He'd been woefully ill-prepared for survival then, without so much as a match to light a fire. He'd spent the night sleepless and shivering under a grove of small trees along the side of the highway.

He was better prepared now, with matches, food, water, and blankets for both of them if they were caught in the open at nightfall. But given a choice, he would choose a house full of mummified corpses over that cold, silent blackness the nights had become any day of the week.

Erik readjusted his backpack to go over both shoulders and Seth fell into step beside him as they returned to the highway.

Ed's Gas & Grocery sat on the west side of the road. To the east was a shallow marsh full of cattails and tall grasses. The forests of north-central Minnesota stretched for miles beyond the marsh and in every other direction. They walked the south-bound lanes of the highway, the dead silence of the marsh and woods around them broken only by the squeaks and scuffs of their sneakers on the pavement.

A little more than half a mile down the road, they came upon a rusty yellow Volkswagen beetle in the ditch to their right. Traveling north the night of the storm, it had rolled across the median and south-bound lanes before crossing into the ditch and stopping a few yards short of the edge of the woods. Erik didn't need to check to know there would be a mummified corpse behind the wheel.

As they passed the car, he couldn't help but wonder if maybe the driver was Emily's husband or fiancé, and if he'd been on his way to pick her up from her late-night shift at the store. If so, and if he'd left a few minutes earlier or driven a little faster, he and Emily could have died together in the same place rather than alone and apart – one on the floor of a lonely little convenience store and the other in a crappy yellow car off the side of the road.

***

"Well, this sucks." Erik glanced down to Seth. "Think we can get through that?"

Seth, staring wide-eyed at the sprawling wreckage in front of them, gave a slow shake of his head.

Highway 169 entered Aitkin from the north and then curved west through town, running parallel to a set of railroad tracks before turning south again. Boxcars, flatbeds, and tanker cars lay jumbled and crushed together all along the tracks. A few were pushed all the way up to and across the highway, plowing dirt, rocks, pavement, and more than a few trees ahead of them.

Erik glanced down the tracks to the west. The wreckage extended all the way into town for as far as he could see. The train had taken out several intersections and a few dozen buildings as well. Two weeks ago, such a massive wreck would have made national news. Now, it was little more than an inconvenience.

He sighed. "We'll have to find a way through it in the morning, I guess. It's getting late."

They backtracked north a bit and then headed west down a residential street. The houses here were older, two-story homes with mature oak, ash, and maple trees in the yards. A few cars and pickup trucks were parked along one side of the street while others sat in their driveways or were hidden away in detached garages.

Though it was only mid-June, the trees had already dropped most of their leaves. Erik guessed it was another effect of the storm. The leaves had turned brown and begun falling within a couple of days, far too quickly to be caused by the decreased sunlight.

The lawns too were dead, as were the flowers in the gardens and window boxes of several of the homes. It looked as though autumn had come early to central Minnesota, but it had skipped the usual red, yellow, and gold colors and gone straight to brown.

Here and there amongst the leaves, he caught sight of dead squirrels, birds, and a few rabbits. Occasionally, he would see a cat and sometimes a dog. Back in Grand Rapids, he'd examined a few of the dead animals and confirmed that they were also mummified. With few exceptions, the storm had been an equal-opportunity killer.

Walking up the center of the street, they passed by the first few houses without stopping. These had bicycles or toys lying abandoned on the front lawns, skateboards in the driveways, or basketball hoops above the garage doors – signs of children or teenagers. Over the past few days, Erik had learned that while Seth had no problem with the dead animals lying about in the streets and yards, he didn't do so well with dead people, especially children. Anytime he saw a dead person, he would do that catatonic-zombie thing again for a few hours until Erik coaxed him out of it.

He picked out a small, single-story house with a brick facade and white shutters on the windows. It looked promising. There was a late-model, tan, four-door Ford in the driveway and a flowerbed along the front of the house that looked like it was well-tended before its untimely demise. Nothing about this home bespoke of children.

While Seth waited on the sidewalk, Erik went up to the front door and knocked. It felt silly, considering he and Seth were quite possibly the last two living people on Earth, but he didn't want to go breaking into a house only to find it occupied by a third survivor.

Getting no reply to his knock, he stepped to the side and peered in through one of the windows. There was no sign of movement inside. Going back to the door, he tried the handle and was not surprised to find it locked. They almost always were. The only doors he'd found unlocked were those of the occasional farmhouse along the highway.

He shrugged off his backpack and pulled out the pry bar again. He had picked it up in a hardware store back in Grand Rapids after nearly breaking his ankle trying to kick a door open like he'd seen in the movies.

He wedged the flat end of the bar between the door and the frame right above the lock. Setting his feet apart, he took a breath, steadied himself, and gave a sudden, violent shove against the bar, putting his weight into it. The door jamb splintered with a loud crack as the deadbolt tore through the wood.

The door swung open.

He waited, listening to see if the racket would bring anyone out of the shadows inside. When no one appeared, he glanced back to Seth and gave him a thumbs-up.

Seth returned the gesture but stayed where he was on the sidewalk. He knew the drill.

Erik went inside and moved quickly through the house, "clearing" it as he'd come to call the routine – scouting for dead bodies, both human and animal, and taking note of the general layout of the home. From the framed pictures of children and young adults in the living room to the general lack of clutter, he was almost sure this was the home of an older couple, grandparents most likely. His suspicions were confirmed when he came to the master bedroom. The mummified remains of an elderly couple lay side by side in their queen-size bed, their ages evident by the partial dentures and reading glasses lying on the bedside tables.

One effect of the storm Erik was thankful for was the lack of decomposition in the mummies. There was no odor of decay or stench of escaping gasses from the bodies. Along with everything else, the storm seemed to have killed off even the bacteria or whatever it was that caused dead bodies to rot and bloat.

He pulled the bedroom door closed and finished his search of the house. When he was satisfied the only corpses in the house were hidden in the bedroom, he went back outside and waved Seth in.

In the kitchen, Erik was surprised to find not only that the house still had running water, but that it also had a gas stove. Scrounging through the pantry, he found cans of beef and vegetable soup, a pack of noodles, and a box of crackers. He mixed the soup and noodles together and heated the mix on the stove. Every house they'd previously stayed in had an electric stove, forcing them to make do with cold dinners.

They ate their first hot meal in days by the light of the gas flames and several candles Seth found in a drawer. When they were done, Erik ran water in the bathtub. He found a large stewpot and used it to heat water on the stovetop to add to the bath. He let Seth go first, then heated more water for himself and soaked in the tub until the water began to cool.

After hot food and a bath, Erik felt better than he had in days. He left a candle burning in the bathroom across from the master bedroom in case either of them had to get up during the night and then joined Seth in the living room where he set up more candles. Seth was sitting on the couch with a book in his lap, turning the pages and looking at the pictures.

"What have you got there, kiddo?" He took a seat on the couch next to the boy and glanced at the cover of the book. It was *The Lorax* by Dr. Seuss. "Where did you get that?"

Without looking up, Seth pointed to a short bookshelf across the room. The top two shelves held thick, hard-cover books while the bottom shelf held an assortment of children's books, jigsaw puzzles, and board games, no doubt for the grandkids.

"That's my sister's favorite book. I think I've read it to her at least a hundred times."

Seth placed the open book in Erik's lap and looked up at him expectantly.

"What? You want me to read it to you?"

Seth nodded vigorously.

Erik gave an exaggerated sigh. "Okay, fine. But we're not going to make a habit of this."

Though he probably could have recited the entire thing from memory, Erik picked the book up, turned back to the first page, and began to read aloud.

As he read and turned the pages, it felt so familiar that his thoughts began stealing back to the days before the storm, before he left for camp, when he would sit with his sister every night and read her a story before bedtime. They would sit crosswise on her bed, their backs to the wall, reading by the light of the lamp on her bedside table. The white and black cat she'd named Spritz would always wander into the room about halfway through the story and curl up on the bed at Sam's feet.

Samantha, or Sam, as everyone called her, was eight years old, with long blonde hair and blue eyes. She would sit right up next to Erik as he read aloud, sometimes leaning in so close to study the pictures that he would have to move the book around so he could keep reading. Dr. Seuss was her favorite author and *The Lorax* and *Horton Hears a Who* were her favorite books.

He had only recently convinced Sam there were other stories besides ones about cats in hats, Whos, and Barbaloots. Before he left for camp, they had begun reading *Alice's Adventures in Wonderland*. As with *The Lorax*, she was completely captivated by both the story and the pictures. He'd promised her they would finish it when he returned home.

After a while, Erik realized he was no longer reading. He was staring at the book but not seeing it. He glanced over and saw that Seth was curled up on the couch next to him, fast asleep. When had that happened? He glanced at the book again and saw he was on the last page. He must have finished it and then completely spaced out on his thoughts of Sam.

Across the room, the windows showed that night had already fallen in all its total darkness.

He closed the book and set it aside, then covered Seth with a blanket from the closet in the hall. He spread out more blankets for himself and stretched out on the floor next to the couch. They never slept in the beds of the houses they stayed in. Even if they found a house with no corpses in it, Erik preferred sleeping on the floor in the living room with Seth on the couch. He felt if he slept in one of the beds, it would somehow imply he was going to stay longer than one night.

Lying on the floor with his hands behind his head, he stared up at the ceiling, watching the flickering shadows thrown off by the candles. He thought of Sam and his promise to return and finish reading *Alice's Adventures in Wonderland* to her.

No, he would not be staying anywhere for any length of time. He had to keep moving. He had to get home. He had a promise to keep.

***

He was sitting on the edge of the deck of their house in Iowa, leaning back on his hands with his bare feet touching the top of the grass. It was a warm, summer day with a slight breeze and a few billowy white clouds drifting slowly across the blue sky. There had been no storm here. Everything was bright and alive.

His mother was at the hospital in Ames where she worked as an emergency room nurse. As usual, she wouldn't be home until late, leaving Erik to look after Sam.

Erik didn't mind babysitting his little sister. He had been looking after her since their father moved out of the house almost five years ago. Sam was never any trouble, and it wasn't as if Erik had any kind of social life, not stuck in a small, rural town of less than three hundred people, only two or three of whom were his own age.

Across the backyard, Sam was crouched on her hands and knees, staring intently at something in the slightly overgrown grass by the garden. Every now and then, she would scoot forward a few feet, never taking her eyes off the caterpillar or beetle or whatever little critter she was stalking. She loved all animals, even the ones other girls and some boys found icky or scary. Millipedes and spiders were of particular fascination to her. The more legs the better.

As she scooted forward on her knees again, Erik tilted his head back and closed his eyes, feeling the warmth of the sun on his face. Sam was wearing her new tights with a bright floral print. Their mother was going to raise holy hell when she came home and saw the grass stains on the knees. Erik would take the heat, as he should have known better than to let Sam play outside in her new clothes, but for now he didn't care. Let Sam have her fun. Grass stains could be washed out. And even if they couldn't, he would buy her a new pair out of his own money. Problem solved.

A tiny yelp from across the yard snapped him out of his thoughts. He looked and saw Sam jumping to her feet, holding her right hand in her left while staring at her index finger. She turned and came running through the grass toward him.

He caught her, lifting her up and setting her on his knee.

"What's wrong?"

She was whimpering, on the verge of crying. He took her hand and looked at her finger.

"It stung me," she said in a tiny voice. Tears were brimming at the corners of her eyes.

"Let me see."

He examined her finger and saw a small, black stinger embedded in the tip. The sting was already beginning to swell a bit.

"You were chasing a bee?"

Sam nodded, sniffing back tears.

"Did you try to pick it up?"

She gave a slight shake of her head, pouting.

"Pet it."

Erik suppressed a grin. Of course, she had been trying to pet it.

"Well, come on then." He stood and picked her up in his arms. "Let's get that stinger out and put some ice on it. But now you know we don't pet bees, right? It's okay to look at them but we don't touch them."

She gave a small whimper as she wrapped her arms around his neck and put her head on his shoulder. Erik knew she was probably more upset about the bee stinging her than she was about the pain. The bee had betrayed her.

He carried her into the house through the door to the kitchen to set her on the counter so he could perform the minor triage. The door slammed shut behind him, banging way too loud.

The entire house shuddered.

Erik sat up and looked around, suddenly wide awake and alert. The candles on the table were burned almost completely down. Seth's blanket lay in a pile on the floor and the couch was empty.

He heard a muffled boom and what sounded like a distant rumble of thunder. The windows rattled and he felt the floor shudder beneath him. The windows across the room were glowing with a shifting, orange-red light from outside.

His first thought was of the storm. His stomach clenched. Was it happening again? Was he about to be turned into one of those dried-up mummies like everyone at camp? Like Emily?

A sound like the mewling of a cat came from the darkened hallway. For a second, he didn't understand what it could be, and then he remembered that Seth wasn't on the couch anymore.

Damn it!

Throwing the blankets aside, he grabbed a candle from the table, and headed quickly for the hallway. The candle had gone out in the bathroom.

Across the hall, the door to the master bedroom stood wide open. The orange glow from outside was coming through the bedroom windows.

Seth was sitting on the floor of the hallway next to the bedroom door, his head down and his arms wrapped around his knees. He was rocking back and forth, crying quietly.

In the bedroom, Erik could see the mummified face of the woman staring back at him, her death-grin and dark eye sockets looking creepy as hell in the flickering orange light.

He went in and pulled the covers up over the corpses. Pulling the door closed behind him, he joined Seth on the floor and put an arm around the boy's thin shoulders.

"Hey, buddy. I think you took a wrong turn. Did you need to use the bathroom?"

Seth made another low mewling noise and nodded his head a little.

"Okay. Come on then. I'll help you." He urged Seth to stand up and then led him across the hall to the bathroom.

He replaced the burned-out candle with the one he carried. When Seth was done, he led him back to the couch. By the time Erik covered him with the blanket again, Seth had stopped crying. Erik sat on the couch next to him and waited until the boy fell asleep again.

He walked to the windows and looked out. The orange glow was coming from the south side of town, maybe a mile away. As he watched, a brilliant ball of red and yellow fire rose into the air. It was followed a second or two later by a muffled boom and the low, rumbling shudder he felt earlier. He wondered if it was a gas main. The explosions and fire looked like ones he'd seen on the news when natural gas lines leaked and then exploded.

He watched as a couple of smaller explosions lit up the sky a minute later and then returned to his makeshift bed on the floor. If it was a gas main, he wondered what could have set it off. There was no electricity to cause a spark and there couldn't have been any lightning strikes due to the complete lack of weather. A mechanical cause also seemed unlikely. He had yet to find even a wind-up watch that still worked.

He pondered on it before drifting off to sleep again. His last thoughts were that, like the train wreck, they were probably in for another detour tomorrow. The explosions and fire looked like they were right along the highway where it led south out of town.

JUNE 25

If Seth remembered anything from the previous night, he didn't show it the next morning. He sat across from Erik at the kitchen table, happily eating a bowl of dry, not-quite-stale kid's cereal Erik found in the pantry. The cereal contained little multi-colored bits shaped like pieces of fruit. The propaganda on the cereal box claimed these colorful bits were marshmallows.

Erik went back to the pantry and found the bag of actual marshmallows he'd seen last night. He took one from the bag and brought it back to the table.

"Marshmallow," he said, setting it in front of Seth. He then placed one of the little, hard, green things from Seth's cereal next to it. He looked from one to the other and then back to Seth. Frowning, he indicated the green thing and shook his head sadly. "Not marshmallow."

Seth studied them both, looked up at Erik, back to the real and fake marshmallows again, and then quickly scooped both up and popped them into his mouth. He laughed soundlessly as he chewed.

Erik sighed and shook his head. Kids didn't care if they were eating flavored cardboard or not, as long as it was sweet and colorful. He went back to eating the toaster pastries he had heated up for himself over the stove.

After breakfast, Erik made sure their water bottles were topped off from the kitchen faucet and added a few items from the pantry to his backpack. Seth disappeared into the living room and returned with *The Lorax*.

"You're killing me here," Erik said. But he took the book anyway and slid it into his pack.

Rather than backtrack east to where they'd left the highway, they continued west along the street, staying parallel to the highway and railroad tracks. Thick smoke was still rising from the south, adding to a spreading, toxic, black cloud hanging low over that part of the city. Erik thought it looked like a giant oil slick in the sky.

After a couple of blocks, they turned south again. Erik planned to reconnect with the highway where it also turned south and then crossed the east-west railroad tracks. He hoped it would be easier to find a safe way through the wreckage at the crossing.

As they came up to a small city park on their left, Erik suddenly turned Seth around before the boy could see what he'd just seen. He led Seth back up the street a few hundred feet or so, glanced back to make sure the park was out of sight, and then steered him to a large oak tree next to the road. He dug into his pocket and pulled out the little metal Corvette he'd picked up at Ed's Gas & Grocery. He'd all but forgotten about it.

"Hey, kiddo. I got this for you back at that gas station. Why don't you stay here and play with this for a few minutes while I go up and check something out? I'll be right back."

Seth happily accepted the toy and sat on the ground, driving the car silently around the patch of bare dirt at the base of the tree.

Erik headed back down the street to the park and then stopped and stared, trying to make sense of what he was seeing.

In the middle of the park was a large cottonwood tree unaffected by the storm, as was the patch of grass about fifty feet in diameter below it. The tree was alive and full of leaves. The grass was lush and green.

Sitting at the base of the tree, a little off to the side but still on the green grass, sat a large, wooden, dining room table surrounded by six high-back chairs. The table was set for a fancy dinner party, complete with candlesticks, plates, bowls, silverware, wine glasses, and cloth napkins. The plates and bowls held an assortment of dead birds, squirrels, chipmunks, and other small animals. A large serving platter in the center of the table held a dead raccoon and a black and white cat.

In each chair sat a mummified corpse. There were three men and three women. Two of the men were dressed in suits and ties while all the women were in evening wear and jewelry. The third man, the corpse at the head of the table, was wearing a tuxedo and top hat. He had one arm outstretched over the table, wine glass in hand, as though he was proposing a toast. In the wine glass was a dead rat.

Erik walked slowly around the bizarre tableau, taking it all in. It was the most outrageous thing he'd ever seen. It was strange, creepy, and a little unsettling. He didn't know what to think but he seriously doubted these people would have been having a formal dinner party in the park at two in the morning on a Sunday. They didn't die here. Someone set this up. And whoever had done it either had a morbid sense of humor or was possibly insane.

He glanced around at the houses surrounding the park, now acutely aware of all the darkened windows in them. He felt a crawling sensation up his spine. There was someone else alive in this town. Were they watching him now, maybe gauging his reaction to their work of apocalyptic art?

He felt exposed, as though he himself was on display. He turned and left the park as quickly as he could without running, resisting the urge to glance back over his shoulder.

Seth was still under the oak tree playing with his car. Erik slowed his pace and walked up to him as though he'd simply gone up the road to make sure it wasn't snowing or anything.

"Hey, kiddo," he said casually. "Let's get rolling. We still have to find a way through that train wreck, you know."

Seth stood and pocketed the toy, falling in alongside Erik as they headed west again, away from the park and away from the dinner party for the dead.

***

Erik studied the pile of train cars blocking the street in front of them. As he'd guessed yesterday, the wreck extended all the way through town. Some of the cars had plowed through the houses and buildings on either side of the tracks, demolishing everything in their path.

Seth, also studying the wreck, pointed to an empty boxcar sitting crosswise on the tracks, both of its side doors open. A tanker car was crushed up against it, partially blocking the door on this side, but it still looked passable.

"Good job, kiddo," Erik said, mussing his hair. "You think you can climb through that?"

Seth cocked his head and gave the cars a little more scrutiny before glancing back up at Erik. He gave a single, affirmative nod.

"Okay, but we need to take it slow. If those suckers start to shift on us, we'll be squashed like bugs."

He helped Seth climb up into the boxcar and then followed him. The inside was coated with a fine layer of dust and they had to step carefully on the tilted floor to keep from sliding all the way through. Reaching the other door, he lowered Seth to the ground and then jumped down himself. He brushed himself off and high-fived Seth.

They followed the street up a small hill, now running parallel to the highway as it headed south again. At the top of the hill, they turned east and headed through a small neighborhood of newer, single-story houses.

Seth, feeling confident after successfully navigating them through the wreckage of the train, led the way, staying a few steps ahead of him. Erik was about to tell him not to get too far ahead when he was brought up short by a voice calling from behind them.

"You probably don't want to go that way."

Erik stopped and whirled around. On the front porch of a house they had just passed, a boy about his own age was getting up from a wicker rocking chair. He stepped to the porch railing and leaned forward on it. He was a little shorter than Erik but stockier, with close-cut brown hair and brown eyes. He had a bottle of beer in one hand and an easy grin on his face.

"There's a little historic graveyard up that way," the boy said, pointing up the road with his beer bottle. "Probably has only fifty or so graves in it. But if you thought that shit in the park was fucked up, you definitely don't want to see what he did up there."

Erik stared at him without saying anything. The boy must have been sitting there, watching them approach and then walk right past until he decided to announce himself. He felt Seth come up beside him.

"Booga booga!" the boy shouted, waving his arms at them before laughing. "No, I ain't no fucking ghost. You gonna stand there gawking or are you gonna say something? Come on up and take a load off. I'm not going to kill you."

Erik glanced down at Seth. What else could they do? This was the first living person either of them had seen for two weeks. He gave Seth a "why not?" shrug. Seth shrugged back in the same manner and then followed close beside him as they backtracked to the house and joined the boy on the porch.

"Man, I couldn't believe it when I saw you guys coming up the street," the boy said, shaking Erik's hand. "Thought you were that crazy bastard at first but then I saw there were two of you. Name's Tyler, by the way. You want a beer? It's warm but I've got plenty." He indicated the open case of beer on the floor next to the rocker. "Got a bunch of wine and booze too. Just name your poison."

Erik shook his head. "A little early for me." He introduced himself and Seth.

Tyler held his hand out to Seth, who stared at the outstretched hand and studied it before tentatively reaching out his own. Tyler grabbed Seth's hand in both of his and shook it firmly.

"Atta boy, little dude."

Seth cast a quick, nervous smile to Erik before Tyler let go of his hand. Erik put his hand on Seth's shoulder and gave it a reassuring squeeze.

"So, who were you talking about?" Erik asked. He shrugged out of his backpack and set it on the floor of the porch. "There's someone else in town? And how did you know we came by way of the park?"

"Just a guess," Tyler said. "Figured since you were coming up that road there, you must have gone by the park." He leaned back on the railing. "And, yeah, there's one other person in town that I know of. He's a tall, skinny guy, shaved head and scraggly beard, covered with tattoos, rings in his ears and nose… the works. He likes to wear suspenders with no shirt." He shrugged. "I don't know his name. I call him Crazy Bob. He's the one who did that fucked-up display in the park."

"Is he dangerous?"

Tyler shrugged again. "Don't know. I stay out of his way. I don't think he even knows I'm here. He's a crazy bastard though. He carries at least two guns all the time. I hear shots every now and then, different places around town. Don't know what he's shooting at but at least it's not me." He tipped the beer bottle to his lips, drained it, and then casually tossed it over the railing and into the yard.

"How do you avoid him?"

"Mostly, I wait until I hear him shooting something up, then I go the other way. He cleaned out the local pharmacy, so I figure he's pretty high on drugs most of the time. He also likes to burn and blow things up. He must have found a bunch of dynamite or something somewhere. If you'd come down Main Street, you would have seen what's left of the police station and courthouse. Those explosions last night? Bet you a piss-warm beer that was him blowing up the truck stop on the highway south of here."

"Yeah, I saw that last night. We were up on the north end of town. I thought it was a gas main or something." He remembered what Tyler had said when he stopped them. "So, what's up the road here at the cemetery?"

Tyler shook his head. "Not anything you'd want the kid to see. Let's just say the park is PG-13. What he did at the cemetery? That shit is X-rated. And not all the bodies are human, if you know what I mean."

"No, that probably wouldn't be good," Erik agreed, trying to keep his imagination from getting too creative. "Seth has kind of a problem around corpses, mostly the people variety. I steered him away from the park."

"Yeah, Crazy Bob's definitely got a twisted sense of humor. But, if nothing else, he keeps things interesting around here. You sure you don't want a beer or something? I've got a bunch more inside. Beer, wine, whiskey, vodka… pretty much an open bar these days."

Erik declined again. He'd tasted wine and beer before. Both were okay but he'd never seen the attraction.

"Suit yourself," Tyler said. "But in case you haven't heard yet, prohibition's been lifted. No more age restrictions." He glanced to Seth. "Except for you, little man. How old are you?"

"He doesn't talk," Erik said.

"No shit? Is he your brother?"

"No, but we're kind of traveling together. Found him up in Hill City."

"Hill City? Jesus, that's like thirty, forty miles away. You walked all the way here?"

Erik shrugged. "It's not that bad. Do a few miles every day. A couple weeks later, here we are."

"Where are you headed?"

"Iowa."

Tyler looked impressed. "Damn! You guys set the bar high. Here, I've been sitting on my ass since… since whenever this shit all went down." He glanced back toward the road. "I was figuring the Marines or someone would have shown up by now, at least some goddamn news reporters wanting to know what the hell happened." He sighed. "Guess that ain't happenin' though, huh?" He pushed himself off the railing. "You guys want to come in or are you on a tight schedule?"

"Well, I was hoping to make the three-fifteen bus," Erik joked, looking at the non-existent watch on his wrist, "but I think we can spare a few minutes. What do you think, kiddo?"

Seth glanced at his own non-existent wristwatch and then back up to Erik. He nodded once.

***

Tyler had become somewhat of a hoarder. Boxes and bags of food crowded the kitchen counters. Cases of beer, wine, and liquor were stacked three high in the living room. There were lanterns and bottles of fuel in every room. Hard cover books, paperbacks, and comic books littered the couches, tables, and floors throughout the house. Erik noticed that Tyler had also accumulated quite a collection of pornographic magazines.

"What can I say?" Tyler said as he gave them a quick tour of the house. "Not much to do these days except hoard food, drink, read, and spank the monkey a couple times a day." He casually scooped up the porn magazines ahead of Seth as they moved from room to room and stashed them on top of the entertainment center in the living room.

"I'm thinking you don't want to be explaining the birds and the bees to the kid yet," he said to Erik, grinning.

Tyler also collected up the comic books. These he handed to Seth.

"Here you go, little dude. Knock yourself out."

Seth set the comics on the couch and then crawled up next to them. He took the first comic off the stack and began leafing through it.

"So, is this your house or did you, like, commandeer it?" Erik asked as he and Tyler went back to the kitchen. Erik sat at the table while Tyler scrounged in an overhead cabinet for something.

"My house," Tyler said. "I guess it's mine now, by inheritance anyway." He pulled out two wine glasses and set them on the table, then took an open bottle of red wine from the counter and filled both glasses.

"You're not getting out of here without having a drink. House rules."

Tyler took a seat at the table opposite Erik and lifted his glass in a toast. "*Gut dich ze treffen.*"

Erik paused in the middle of raising his own glass.

"Say what?"

"Good to meet you," Tyler said. "It's German."

"Ah…" Erik returned the toast and they both sipped the wine. It had a mild, oaky flavor.

"Blame my grandfather," Tyler said. "He never took me fishing or anything but he sure seemed determined to teach me German. I think he secretly thought the Nazis were going to rise again and knowing how to speak German might someday save my ass."

"We probably don't have to worry about that anymore, or the south rising again for that matter."

Tyler took another drink. "So, have you seen anyone else? Anyone alive?"

"Just Seth. And now you. Other than that, nothing but mummified corpses. I don't think even the insects made it. You know, I haven't seen so much as a fly or been bitten by a single mosquito since the storm."

Tyler considered this. "I never even thought about that. But, shit, you're right. No mosquitoes, no flies, no lady bugs... nothing. There's that tree in the park. You know, the one Crazy Bob set up that table under. And the grass. I've seen a couple other patches of green here and there around town. But damn! If you haven't seen anyone since Grand Rapids, I'm thinking we're pretty much fucked."

"Yeah, that's kind of what I've been thinking too. I hung out in Grand Rapids for about three days, waiting for the helicopters to arrive and a bunch of guys in white suits to jump out and start bagging up the bodies and taking samples. When no one showed up, I decided to head south. After the first couple of towns, I gave up looking for other survivors and decided to keep going until I reached home."

"What about the kid? What's the story there?"

"I ran across him up in Hill City. He was sitting on the steps in front of a house, staring straight ahead. He was pretty much a zombie. I couldn't get him to talk or anything. I went into the house and everyone in it was dead – mother, father, brother, even the dog and a couple of birds in a cage. I figure he probably woke up the morning after the storm, found his whole family reduced to mummies, and went into shock or something. I finally got him to eat and drink but I had to lead him along like a dog for a while when we left." He shrugged. "He's making progress but he still hasn't said a word. I'm kind of wondering if he'll ever talk again."

"Are you taking him all the way to Iowa with you?"

"I guess so. I mean, I can't leave him to starve. At first, I was kind of hoping I'd come across a town somewhere with a group of survivors, someplace I could drop him off and then keep going. But I don't know. He's not much trouble and he does sort of keep me company. I guess I could take him with me all the way to Iowa."

Tyler chuckled. "You had to lead him around, he's not much trouble, and he keeps you company. Sounds like you've got yourself a puppy."

Erik smiled himself at the thought. "Well, now that you mention it…"

Tyler leaned back in his chair, crossed his arms, and sighed.

"Shit. I don't know what I'm going to do. I've been sitting around here since…" He waived his hand in the air. "Since whatever the fuck happened."

"The storm."

Tyler leaned forward again, frowning. "You mentioned that before. What storm?"

"The storm. The thing that did all this, that killed everyone. It wasn't like a real storm, you know, like a thunderstorm. It's just the only thing I can think to call it."

"What? You saw it?"

Erik nodded. "Yeah, it was a little after two o'clock in the morning. I was at a camp north of Grand Rapids. My watch stopped at two-seventeen and every other clock I've come across stopped at about the same time."

"So, what the hell happened?" Tyler asked, eager to hear the story. "What did you see?"

Erik drained the rest of the wine in his glass and leaned back in his chair before speaking.

JUNE 7
(TWO WEEKS EARLIER)

Erik felt around on the floor of the tent next to his pillow until he found his wristwatch. He picked it up and held it close to his face, pressing the button on the crown to make it light up. He squinted and read the time – 2:15.

Crap.

He dropped his hand and groaned. He hated having to get up in the middle of the night to take a piss.

He rolled over, trying to ignore his bladder and will himself back to sleep. But Conner, his tent-mate in the sleeping bag across from him, was snoring again. After a few minutes he gave up. Now he was too annoyed to sleep.

He unzipped his sleeping bag and crawled out of the tent. It was cool and dew was on the grass. It was a clear night with no moon but the stars provided enough light for him to see to the edge of the woods. The campfire from several hours earlier had burned down and was now a pile of glowing embers. A half-dozen other tents sat with his, all clustered around the dead fire on this shore of the lake.

The latrines were up the hill next to the administration building and storage shed, but to heck with that. The tree line was closer and all he had to do was take a piss. Barefoot, he made his way through the pine needles, cool sand, and wet grass to the nearest tree.

As he relieved himself against the tree, Erik thought anyone who talked about the stillness of the woods at night must never have been in the woods at night. From deep in the trees came the hooting of an owl and the distant yipping and howling of coyotes. Closer to the camp, bullfrogs were thrumming and crickets were chirping. The eerie call of a loon came from somewhere across the lake.

Far from being quiet, still, and peaceful, the woods were a pretty noisy, busy place after the sun went down.

Shaking off the last drops, Erik tucked himself back into his boxers and was turning back to his tent when a brilliant, silent flash of light lit up the sky behind him. For a second or two, he could clearly see his shadow and the shadows of the trees on the ground in front of him.

Startled, he turned and looked in the direction of the flash. It was already over but there was still a bright, greenish glow over the entire western horizon, as though the sun had changed color and was rising early on the wrong side of the planet.

As the glow began to fade, it was replaced by tall, undulating curtains of red, pink, and green lights that quickly spread across the night sky. He thought it looked like the northern lights on steroids.

Fascinated, he watched as the whole sky was enveloped by these fast-moving curtains of brilliant light. Then came the roar of rushing wind and he was hit by the shockwave of whatever had happened. He ducked and turned away before being knocked to his hands and knees by a hot, gale-force wind. Twigs, leaves, dirt, and other forest debris peppered his back. Trees bent and limbs cracked in the woods. He felt more than heard a deep rumbling in the ground beneath him.

It lasted fifteen or twenty seconds, and then the wind died as quickly as it began. The rumbling beneath his hands and feet stilled and everything became eerily quiet.

Erik opened his eyes and cautiously got to his feet. He looked back up at the sky. The curtains of light were fading as they disappeared over the eastern horizon. There were a few flashes of lightning high up in the sky but they didn't last long. After another minute or so, the glow to the west faded and the curtains of light ran their course. The stars returned but seemed a bit dimmer now, a little more pale.

What in the hell was that?

He looked around, aware of the sudden silence of the woods. The flash, the wind, the rumbling – whatever had happened, it had sure shut the forest critters up. He figured they were all probably hiding in their burrows and nests right now, as puzzled as he was.

A few smaller tree limbs and branches lay on the ground, along with a lot of leaves, twigs, and pinecones. Surprisingly, none of the tents had been blown into the lake. He waited a couple of minutes but no one poked their heads out, curious about the short but violent storm. Maybe it hadn't lasted long enough to wake anyone up.

Making his way back to his own tent, Erik ducked in and crawled back into his sleeping bag. He would have to ask one of the camp counselors tomorrow morning if there was anything on the news about it. He wondered if a meteor had hit somewhere to the west. If it was a meteor, it had been a hell of a big one. Or, who knew? Maybe someone had nuked North Dakota.

Punching his pillow to fluff it up, he lay on his side and closed his eyes, settling back down to sleep.

If nothing else, at least Conner had finally stopped snoring.

JUNE 25
(CONTINUED)

Erik drained the wine in his glass again and set it down. Tyler had refilled it at least twice, maybe three times as he'd been talking. He'd stopped counting.

"The next morning, I woke up and was looking right over at Conner. He was still in his sleeping bag, facing me. He was my first mummy. It scared the hell out of me. Then I thought someone was playing a joke. You know? Like someone put a fake corpse in Connor's sleeping bag to scare me. I went outside but didn't see anyone. At first, I thought no one else was awake yet. Then I got the feeling that something wasn't quite right. The woods and the lake were way too quiet. I'd never seen the surface of the lake so still. It was like glass. The sky was gray and hazy like it is now. There was no wind, nothing."

He paused and took a breath, remembering that first morning.

"The sky, the lake... everything felt wrong. I peeked inside one of the other tents, hoping everyone was still sleeping. They were dead too – mummies. All the tents were like that. That's when I started realizing this wasn't a joke. Everyone was dead. I freaked out a little and ran up to the administration building, shouting and hollering. A couple of the counselors stayed up there. They were as dead as everyone else. I tried the phone, the radio, the TV... Nothing worked."

"Never a cop or electrician around when you need one," Tyler quipped.

"After I convinced myself that I was awake and this wasn't a nightmare, I headed up the road to see if I could find help. No one answered their doors when I knocked. I went all the way to Grand Rapids, about twelve miles down the road. There was a truck rolled over in the ditch with a mummy in it. I eventually figured out everyone in town was dead and that no one was coming to help. After a few days, I headed south, ran across Seth, and now here we are."

Tyler had refilled their glasses again. Erik couldn't remember if this was their second bottle of wine or their third. Whatever bottle it was, he no longer cared. He had stopped sipping at the wine a while ago and was now a little beyond being buzzed.

"Man, that's fucked up," Tyler said. "It's like I kind of wish I'd seen it too, the storm. But, then again, I'm also glad I missed it."

"It was... I don't know, a little scary but exhilarating at the same time. That's the best I can describe it."

"Could it have been an atomic bomb or something? Some kind of attack? Like you said, maybe somebody nuked us."

"That's what I wondered at first but it was way too big. That flash and the glow, it was like the whole other side of the world was on fire. Those lights went all the way across the sky, clear to the other horizon. And that lightning way up in the sky... and the hot wind and the rumbling... Man, if that was a weapon of some kind, it had to be some secret doomsday thing."

He paused again, thinking, and then said, "I think whatever it was, it happened on the other side of the world, at least way over the horizon. Maybe we got hit with, I don't know, the side effects."

Tyler leaned back in his chair. "Some side effects! But it makes you wonder, doesn't it? Are we the lucky ones, or are we the damned?"

"I don't know. I guess we'll just have to wait and see."

They had been talking for several hours and the day was quickly heading toward darkness. Tyler lit the lanterns in the kitchen and living room. Seth, still engrossed in his comic books, barely looked up when they walked in.

"So why are you heading to Iowa?" Tyler asked, setting himself in the recliner next to the couch. He had brought the wine in with him and placed it on the coffee table. "I know that's where you're from but do you think your folks are still alive?"

Erik sat on the couch next to Seth.

"I don't know. But *we're* still alive. So, I guess I have to figure there's a chance my mom and sister are alive too. I suppose I could stay up here but then I'd never know for sure."

"I already know," Tyler said morosely. "I buried them in the backyard last week."

They were both quiet for a while before Tyler suddenly sat forward and raised his glass.

"You know what? Fuck the storm and the corpses and all that other shit. It's the end of the world, man! We made it. We win!"

JUNE 26

Erik awoke later than usual the next morning with his first hangover. Seth was already awake and sitting on the couch thumbing through a thick book he'd found somewhere that contained a collection of comic strips about a boy and a tiger. The sound of snoring from down the hall told him that Tyler was still very much asleep.

He rummaged through the cabinets in the kitchen until he found a bottle of ibuprofen and helped himself to a couple. Then he dug through the boxes of food until he found some dry cereal without the fake marshmallows, some bagels that were not quite stale, and some margarine and blackberry jam.

He and Seth were still eating breakfast when Tyler shuffled into the kitchen about twenty minutes later. Erik tossed him the bottle of pills.

Clutching the bottle in his fist, Tyler dropped heavily into one of the chairs and stared blankly at the roadmap spread out on the kitchen table. When he looked up again, he squinted at Erik with bloodshot eyes.

"So, what's the plan? You two bugging out today?"

"Yep," Erik said. "Keep moving forward. That's always the plan. I figure we should be able to make it to Bennettville if we leave early enough." He chewed the last bite of his bagel and washed it down with apple juice. Brushing his hands together, he asked, "You want to stay here and keep spanking the monkey while waiting for the Marines, or do you want to come with us?"

Tyler gazed around the kitchen, eyeing the stacks of boxes and empty wine bottles.

"What, and leave all this?" He looked back to Erik and gave a disgusted snort. "In a fucking heartbeat."

Tyler swallowed some ibuprofen, ate half a dry bagel, and then dug a backpack out of the closet to fill with food and supplies. The way Seth stared at their backpacks prompted Tyler to retrieve a smaller pack from the basement for him. They put some food and juice boxes in it along with a blanket, a few of Tyler's comic books, and the book of comic strips Seth had been looking at that morning. Erik and Tyler each also packed additional fuel for lanterns, matches, lighters, and whatever else they thought they might need and could still stuff into the packs.

When they were ready, Tyler took the time to go to the backyard and stand over his parents' graves for a few minutes. If he said anything, it was too low for Erik to hear as he stood by the side of the house with Seth.

"You sure about this?" he asked when Tyler finished and joined them. "This train ain't stopping until it gets to Iowa."

"I'm sure. There's nothing left for me here anyway. If I stay, I'll probably end up becoming an alcoholic and dying in my own piss and puke. Or Crazy Bob will find me and go all *Deliverance* on my ass."

Erik had never seen the movie but understood the reference.

They started off down the road, detouring around the cemetery and joining up with highway 169 a few blocks farther south. The heavy black cloud still hung over the city but the column of smoke feeding it had gotten noticeably lighter since yesterday.

As they got closer to the edge of town, Tyler's depressed mood lifted a little. Erik figured it was either because they were getting farther from Tyler's house and the graves of his parents, or the ibuprofen was beginning to work on his hangover.

A half-mile south of town, they came upon the source of the smoke. Tyler was right. A truck stop on the east side of the road had been reduced to a pile of smoldering rubble, with shattered concrete walls and twisted steel beams rising out of the ashes. Several semi-trailer trucks that had been parked in the lot were now little more than charred shells. The area where the gas and diesel pumps had once stood was now a ragged, smoking crater about eighty feet across and twenty feet deep.

"Man," Tyler said, "that crazy fucker sure did a number on this place. Good thing he didn't have access to anything bigger, like cruise missiles or a nuclear warhead."

There were large hunks of debris scattered in a wide area, including all over the highway. As they were making their way past the crater and around the blackened chunks of concrete, smoldering wood, and twisted steel, Seth suddenly grabbed tight to Erik's leg, nearly tripping him.

He looked down at Seth and then to where the boy was staring. About twenty feet up the road was a speed limit sign. Propped up against the signpost was what Erik first took to be just another large hunk of burned debris blasted from the truck stop. But a second look told him it was no such thing.

"Oh shit," Tyler said, looking to where Erik and Seth were both staring. "That's not what I think it is, is it?"

It was the blackened body of a man sitting on the ground, his back against the signpost.

"Think he's alive?" Erik asked.

"I don't see how. Shit. Look at him. He's a fucking briquette."

The man's head slowly turned toward the sound of their voices. His eyes were open – two white orbs in a completely blackened face.

"Fuck," Tyler whispered. "He *is* alive."

Erik told Seth to stay put while he and Tyler approached the man.

His clothes were mostly gone and every inch of his exposed skin was blackened and peeling, sometimes deep enough to show the raw, oozing tissue beneath. Patches of skin were missing from his head and Erik could see the dull white sheen of his skull in several places. The man's ears were burned off, his nose and lips were completely gone, and his right hand was nothing more than a blackened nub at the end of a wrist. He still had his left hand but that one was missing all but two of its fingers.

Erik couldn't understand how the man was still alive.

"Is he the crazy guy you were telling me about?" he asked in a low voice. They were standing about five feet from the burn victim.

"Pretty sure it is. Look, you can still see the remains of his suspenders. They're melted into his shoulders. He must have been a little too close to the station when it went up."

Erik leaned in a little closer to the man.

"Can you talk?"

The burned man, whom Tyler had nicknamed Crazy Bob, stared at them for a few seconds. Then, with what appeared to be great effort, he moved his head slightly to the left and then back to the right.

"I think that's a 'no,'" Tyler said.

"Man, he's got to be in a lot of pain. Do you want some water?"

Bob struggled to shake his head again.

"There's not much else we can do for you," Tyler said. "There's no 9-1-1 service anymore and I haven't seen any priests around to give you last rites. Do you want us to just leave you alone and let you die in peace?"

He turned his head a little and seemed to make a point of staring down at the side of the road to Erik's right. Erik followed his gaze, stepped over, and retrieved what the man had been looking at. It was a revolver.

"Is this what you want?"

He nodded.

"What the hell do you want your gun for?" Tyler asked him. "You don't have any hands left."

Erik looked the revolver over. It still appeared functional, though its wood grip was charred almost to nothing. Checking the cylinder, he could see it still had two unspent shells in it.

"I think," Erik said, "he wants one of us to end his suffering."

Tyler looked at the revolver and then back to Bob. "Is that what you want, one of us to do it for you, put a bullet in your head? Put you out of your misery?"

Bob closed his eyes and nodded.

Erik looked at Tyler. "I don't know, man. All I've ever shot are tin cans and paper targets. I've never even been hunting."

"That's still more experience than I have. I used my uncle's shotgun to shoot a few clay pigeons last summer – missed more than I hit – but I've never killed anything either. I've never even used a pistol."

Erik turned the gun over in his hand again, studying it, considering. He knew how to handle guns of all types. As the son of a cop, his father had given him more gun-handling and shooting lessons than a drill sergeant. But as he'd told Tyler, he had never shot anything that was alive. The only living things he'd ever killed were flies, mosquitos, and the occasional spider with a bit of rolled up paper.

He felt Bob's eyes on him again. The man desperately wanted his suffering to end but he couldn't do it himself. If they walked away right now, he would probably be dead by tonight, but it would be slow and agonizing. Erik considered what if it was himself sitting there against that signpost, unable to move, most of his flesh burned away, but still breathing and in unbearable pain.

He glanced back down the road. Seth was still standing where they'd left him, watching them.

"Jesus, you're not thinking of conning the kid into doing it, are you?" Tyler asked.

"No," Erik said slowly, having made up his mind. "I was just thinking. I'll do it. But you need to take Seth a little ways down the road. I don't think it would be good for him to see this."

"Will he go with me? I mean, he seems pretty attached to you."

Erik turned and walked back to Seth, slipping the pistol under his belt behind his back. Tyler followed.

He knelt on one knee in front of Seth and put his hands on the boy's shoulders.

"You need to go with Tyler down the road a ways. I'm going to stay behind and help that man. I'll catch up with you in a few minutes. Okay?"

Seth stared at him, glanced up at Tyler, and then looked back to Erik. He nodded. The look on his face told Erik the boy understood more of what was going on than they gave him credit for.

"Okay." Erik stood up. To Tyler, he said, "Maybe when you get over that little hill up there, it will muffle the sound a bit. I'll wait until you're on the other side."

Tyler gave a brief nod and took Seth's hand.

"Come on, little dude. Let's do like the bear and go shit over the mountain."

Erik waited until they disappeared over the hill, then he went back to Bob – Crazy Bob – sitting against the signpost. He pulled the pistol out and checked the cylinder again to make sure a live round would rotate into position when he cocked it.

He took a deep breath and let it out.

"You're sure you want me to do this?"

This time Bob gave two nods of his head.

"Do you want time to say a prayer or anything?"

Bob managed what Erik could only guess was either a grimace or a rueful grin, followed by a bare shake of his head.

Erik thumbed the hammer back and watched the cylinder rotate, placing a live round in line with the hammer. He held the gun a few inches away from Bob's forehead, but Bob turned his head so the pistol was aimed at his temple.

That made sense. In the forehead, the bullet could go between the two halves of his brain, doing major damage but not killing him immediately. Through the temple, it would go through both halves.

Erik's heart was thudding in his chest. His hand, the gun, and Bob's head were in sharp, crystal clear focus. Everything else faded into the background.

"Ready?" he asked. His mouth had gone dry and the word came out a bit choked. He couldn't believe he was about to do this. It seemed… surreal.

Bob responded by closing his eyes and giving one last nod.

Erik took a deep breath and then let it out slowly.

As his finger was squeezing the trigger, he closed his own eyes. He had never shot a gun with his eyes closed before. Somehow, not seeing the pistol seemed to amplify the sound of the gunshot. It startled him. The pistol recoiled in his hand and he could hear the echoes of the shot reverberating between the buildings of the town behind him. The echoes seemed to last forever.

He took another deep breath and opened his eyes again. Bob had slumped to his side, away from the signpost, and now lay face down on the ground. The post he had been leaning against was spattered with flecks of brain and bone and dripping with blood. Bob, or whatever his real name had been, was most definitely dead. His suffering had ended in a fraction of a second.

Erik's stomach churned and he thought he was going to throw up. He dropped the pistol to the ground and turned away, leaning forward with his hands on his knees and taking deep breaths.

When the nausea passed, he straightened, took another slow, deep breath, and started down the road again to rejoin Tyler and Seth. He didn't look back.

He thought what bothered him the most was not that he had killed a man, but that there were so few people left in the world now, and he had just reduced that number by one.

***

By noon, or what Erik guessed was noon based on the dim spot in the haze above, Tyler was lagging behind, more shuffling and stumbling than walking.

Since leaving Aitkin, they had been going more or less steadily for almost four hours. There had been a little conversation at first but, as the miles dragged on, Tyler had begun conserving more and more of his breath for walking. As they crested the top of another hill, he stopped and leaned forward with his hands on his knees.

"Okay, I give up," he wheezed. "I'll admit it. You fuckers are in better shape than me. I need a fucking rest." He dropped to his knees, shrugged his backpack off, and flopped down spread-eagle on his back in the middle of the highway.

"You wuss." Erik shrugged his own backpack off. He took a bottle of water out and then used the pack as a seat. He took a drink and held the bottle out to Tyler.

"Don't drink too much or you'll cramp up as soon as we start walking again. You'll probably puke too."

Tyler took the bottle and held it against his chest while he continued catching his breath. His shirt was soaked and sweat was running off his forehead despite the mild temperature of the air.

Seth followed Erik's example, also using his backpack as a seat after taking a juice box out. He poked the straw into the box and sucked on it, staring curiously at Tyler.

"Damn," Tyler gasped, still lying on his back. "Who knew walking could be so much work? Especially these fucking hills."

"You'll get used to it in a day or two. Just have to get back to your cave man roots. They walked everywhere, clear across continents even."

"Bullshit. They drove cars and rode dinosaurs and shit. I saw it on *The Flintstones*."

Erik chuckled. "You do realize, don't you, that was a cartoon and not a documentary?"

"Don't care. Same difference."

After another minute or two, Tyler managed to push himself into a sitting position and took a couple drinks of water.

"Speaking of foot power, why in hell aren't we riding bicycles? I know all the cars and machines are dead, but I'm pretty sure bicycles still work."

"Sorry, no can do." Erik patted his right hip. "Fell out of a tree when I was about six years old. Shattered my hip joint. I was in a wheelchair for a good six months and then had to use crutches the rest of that year. I can walk alright now, can even run a bit if I need to. But if I ride a bike or a horse or anything like that, where I'm in a sitting position, I get this god-awful pain that shoots all the way up my back. It's like someone is running a white-hot wire up my spine." He shrugged. "The doctor said it's probably nerve damage. Something about the angle my leg and hip make."

"And you called *me* a wuss? Fucking tough it out, you big baby."

"Would if I could. Wish I could. But it doesn't work."

Tyler took a long swig of water and handed the bottle back to Erik. "How much farther we got?"

"Four or five miles to Bennettville." He looked up at the sky again. "Not sure we're going to make it by dark at this rate."

Tyler struggled to his feet and groaned. He put his hands on his lower back, stretching.

"And you're going all the way to Iowa? How far is that, according to your handy-dandy Ranger Rick map?"

"From here? I'm not sure – four hundred miles, maybe a little more. It was four hundred eighty-two miles from where I started at that camp north of Grand Rapids."

"Are you serious? Over four hundred miles? Jesus! You've been at this for over two weeks now and you haven't even gone a hundred miles yet. That's going to take two or three months."

Erik shrugged. "It's not like I've got anything better to do."

Tyler picked up his backpack and pulled it over his shoulders.

"That's a long fucking way. I don't know. If we come across a group of survivors or some remnant of civilization, I may jump ship on you and stay there. Send me a postcard when you catch your white whale, Ahab."

He adjusted the straps of his backpack and looked at both Erik and Seth still sitting on theirs. "Well come on. You guys have rested long enough. Jesus, if I have to keep stopping and waiting on you two slackers, we'll never get anywhere."

Erik stood and slung his backpack over his shoulders.

"You know," he said to Tyler, "I think you swear more than anyone on the planet."

Tyler spread his arms out, taking in the empty highway and woods around them.

"And that means fucking what?"

Erik chuckled again and shook his head but didn't say anything else.

By the time the sky began to darken, they were still a mile or two north of Bennettville. Before the storm, they would have had plenty of time to reach the town and find a place to shelter. But now, once that haze-shrouded sky began to lose light, Erik knew he could count on only twenty or thirty minutes until full darkness.

They detoured off the highway and climbed over a wire fence before making their way across a small, overgrown pasture to an old weather-faded barn. Inside, it smelled of dust, old pigeon droppings, dry wood, and moldy hay. An antique tractor and a few pieces of rusting farm machinery sat forgotten inside. There were empty horse stalls along one side of the barn with a loft above that was filled with more old hay, machine parts, and piles of lumber.

"Christ," Tyler said, sniffing the air. "We're going to get tuberculosis or some other fucking disease in here."

They pushed the doors open on either end of the barn. Even though there hadn't been so much as a breeze since the storm, just having the doors open made the barn feel a little less stale and stuffy.

They cleared out a small area in the center of the dirt floor to set up camp for the night, kicking aside a few dead pigeons, bats, sparrows, and a couple of rats. Erik used some of the old hay and small pieces of wood to build a campfire. It was now near full dark and it took him several fumbling tries to get the fire going.

"I thought all you Boy Scouts needed to do was clap your hands over a pile of twigs to start a fire," Tyler said. He'd laid his blanket out and was now laying back on it, using his backpack as a pillow.

"That's how wizards do it. Or ninjas. Besides, I was never in scouts."

"What about that camp you were in? I figured it was some Boy Scout jamboree thing or whatever the hell they call it."

Erik helped Seth with his blanket and set about spreading his own out.

"Think of it as more of a boot camp for juvenile offenders."

"What?" Tyler sat up on one elbow, grinning. "No shit? You were a juvie?"

"I guess." He pulled some beef sticks and other snacks out of his backpack, passing some to Seth.

"What'd you do?"

"Punched a kid in school. He was being a bully, pushing other kids around. I told him to knock it off and he got all up in my face, poking me, asking me what I was going to do about it. So, I decked him."

"That's it? They sent you to juvie camp for a hallway fight?" Tyler shook his head. "Sounds a bit harsh. All I ever got was detention and an ass whoopin' when I got home."

"Well, I guess I did break his jaw. And when his head went back, it hit the wall pretty hard. Knocked him out. He spent a day or two in the hospital with a concussion."

"Damn! Remind me not to piss you off."

"Yeah," Erik sighed, "it didn't help that his dad was a state senator and my dad was a cop. The senator screamed holly hell and the judge said that, as a cop's kid, I should hold myself to a higher standard or something like that. I got suspended from school for three days and sent to that camp for the summer, plus probation for a year."

"Bet they didn't do anything at all to him, did they?"

"Nope. He had a couple of his buddies swear he'd accidentally bumped into me in the hall, and that I just up and went all batshit crazy on him." He shrugged. "I don't know. He and his buddies avoided me after that and I never had any trouble with him again, so I guess it all worked out."

"What a dick," Tyler said.

There was a sudden rustling and flapping of wings above them and they all looked up. Two pigeons landed on the roofbeams above their heads and began strutting back and forth, bobbing their heads and cooing.

Seth smiled in a soundless laugh and clapped his hands together.

"I'll be damned," Erik said, grinning. "Those are the first birds I've seen since the storm. First live animals of any kind for that matter."

"Yeah, ain't that neat," Tyler grumbled, lying back on his blanket again and crossing his arms behind his head. "And they parked their asses right over us. Now, on top of tuberculosis, we're going to wake up in the morning all covered in pigeon shit."

JUNE 27

Sam hugged her cat close to her chest and pouted.

Spritz, a mostly white cat with a black and brown tail and a W-shaped splotch of the same coloring between his ears, was used to such hugs. He had his eyes half-closed, purring and sucking up his owner's affection.

"I don't want you to go," she said.

Erik got down on one knee in front of her. His mother stood on the sidewalk behind Sam. His father was waiting beside his patrol car on the street.

"I have to," he said. "But it's only for six weeks. I'll be back before you know it."

"Spritz doesn't want you to go."

He smiled. "Spritz doesn't even like me that much."

Sam looked as though she was going to begin crying again.

"It's my fault."

He pulled her to himself and hugged her as best he could with Spritz sandwiched between them.

"Hey, it's not your fault, not even a little. He shouldn't have pushed you and I should have gone to the principal instead of punching him. You didn't do anything wrong. But you know what? I don't think he'll ever push you again. And I'll be home before you know it. Then we can finish reading all about Alice and that silly guy in the hat, okay?"

"Do you promise you'll be back?"

"I promise. I'll come back for you. And if I can't find you, you come find me. Okay?"

She gave a small nod and sniffed.

He gave her another hug.

Spritz reached up with his paw and batted him on the nose.

Erik snapped awake, jerking his head back. A startled pigeon flapped furiously into the air, raising a cloud of moldy dust. He heard the second pigeon also take flight from somewhere down by his feet. The birds disappeared out the open barn door into the hazy light of morning.

He pushed himself up and coughed, batting away the cloud of dust with his hand. He glanced around, rubbing his nose where the bird had pecked it and getting his bearings.

Tyler rolled over in his blanket and grumbled something, disturbed by the noise.

The fire had burned down to a small pile of gray ash. Erik looked to Seth's blanket and saw that it was empty. He quickly glanced around the barn but could see no sign of the boy. He flung his own blanket off and stood, glancing around again. Nothing else was moving in the barn so Seth had to be outside.

He went out the front of the barn and looked out over the overgrown pasture to the fence and highway. Nothing was moving. Turning, he headed back through the barn toward the other door.

"What the hell are you doing?" Tyler asked, sitting up. "Chasing flies? Christ, you're stirring up all the dust."

"Looking for Seth. He's gone."

He went out the back of the barn and looked out over the pasture there. It stretched several hundred yards to another fence line that separated the pasture from the woods. Seth was standing at the fence line beneath the overhanging branches of a large tree. He was stroking the neck of a horse that was standing patiently next to a large, steel watering tank.

Erik approached slowly so as not to spook the horse. He didn't know much about horses but this one looked half-starved. He could clearly see the outline of its spine and all its ribs. It was reddish-brown in color and appeared quite old.

Seth turned his head to him and smiled.

Erik tousled his hair and then joined him in stroking the horse's neck. "Found yourself a friend, huh?" He glanced into the water tank and saw it was empty. A cracked layer of brown mud coated the bottom.

"More like a thousand-pound lawn mower," Tyler said. He had come up from the barn behind Erik.

There was a hydrant next to the tank. Erik lifted the handle and was not surprised when nothing came out. The hydrant was probably connected to a well and powered by an electric pump.

Tyler stroked the horse's nose. "I think he's about two days past dead."

"He'll be dead for sure if we don't get him some water. But I think we can fix that. Hang on."

Erik went back to the barn and found a small, plastic bucket in one of the old horse stalls. He dug all the water bottles out of their backpacks and filled the bucket to almost full. He then carried it back to the fence line.

"We can get more water in the next town," he said. "It's not that far down the road."

He held the bucket under the horse's nose and then slowly lowered it to the ground. The horse followed it and quickly drained the bucket dry.

Erik patted the horse's neck. "We need to let him out of this pasture. He should be able to find more water on his own."

"If he can't, he's either blind or stupid," Tyler said. "You throw a rock anywhere in Minnesota and you'll hit a lake."

Even the small amount of water they'd been able to give it seemed to give the horse new life. It followed them back to the barn, where they gathered their backpacks together and made sure the ashes from last night's fire were completely smothered with dirt.

"I don't think it would be much of a loss if this barn did burn down," Tyler commented as Erik stomped the dirt with his foot.

"Yeah, but with how dry everything is now, do you really want to be outrunning a wildfire for the next two days?"

In the pasture, they looked up and down the fence line for a gate.

"Well how in hell did they get the horse in here?" Tyler asked. "Did they wait until it wandered into the pasture and then quick build the fence around it?"

"Must be on the other side of the pasture."

"Screw that." Tyler dropped his backpack and dug inside it. He pulled out a multi-tool and opened it to the pliers with wire cutters on the jaws. "We'll make our own damn gate."

He went to work on the top strand of barbed wire. The small cutters had obviously not been intended to cut through something that thick. He had to bear down on them, working the jaws back and forth over the wire.

Seth was still petting the horse's neck and Erik was standing behind him when the cutters finally bit through the wire. The strand separated with a loud *twang* and snapped back; all its tension released at once.

The sudden noise startled the horse. It reared back away from the fence, knocking Seth back into Erik. Erik landed hard on his back.

Tyler flung the tool into the air and shook his hand as though he'd touched a live electrical wire.

"God damn that stings!"

Erik groaned. He'd landed on his backpack and it had knocked a little of the wind out of him. He tried rolling over but felt Seth's weight on his legs.

"Hey, kiddo. You've got to get off me." He pushed himself into a sitting position.

Seth was lying on his back across Erik's shins. His eyes were open and staring up at the overcast sky. At first, he thought Seth must have had the wind knocked out of him too, but then he saw the side of the boy's face was streaked with blood.

"Oh shit." Tyler was staring down at Seth, a grimacing look of shock and horror on his face.

Erik quickly pulled his legs out from under Seth and scrambled around to get a closer look. The side of Seth's neck had been ripped open. Blood was pumping out of a ragged gash and flowing into a growing pool of red on the ground. Seth's gaze was fixed on the sky. His lips were working slowly as if he was trying to speak.

"God *damn* it!" Erik threw his backpack off and quickly pulled his t-shirt over his head. He wadded it up and pressed it against the side of Seth's neck.

"Hold on there, buddy. Hold on."

Tyler got over his initial shock and dropped to his knees next to them. He put his hands under Seth's head and lifted gently. "Hang in there, little dude."

Erik kept pressure on Seth's neck, not sure what else to do. In less than a minute his t-shirt was completely saturated with blood. It was squeezing out from between his fingers. He looked into Seth's eyes, expecting to see a mix of fear and confusion. Instead, Seth's face had gone slack, pale, expressionless. His eyes were open but now they were staring at nothing. His lips had stopped trying to speak.

Erik kept the pressure on his neck for a little longer. When he finally pulled the shirt away, blood was still oozing a bit from the deep gash but it had stopped pumping.

Tyler glanced up at Erik, a helpless look in his eyes. "Is he going to be okay? What can we do?"

Erik sat back on his legs, still holding his bloody, wadded-up t-shirt. He opened his hand and let it fall to the ground.

"Nothing," he said. "He's gone."

Tyler looked back down at Seth. Carefully, slowly, he lowered Seth's head to the ground.

"Jesus."

Erik stared blankly at the space between his knees and Seth's lifeless body. It had happened so fast. He was still trying to understand it when Tyler asked, "What happened?"

Erik didn't immediately respond. He continued staring at the ground and then his eyes went back to Seth.

"The wire," he said. "It was too tight. When it snapped back, one of those barbs must have caught him across the neck."

"Shit," Tyler muttered. "I'm sorry, man. I didn't know it would do that."

Erik shook his head. "It wasn't your fault. It wasn't anyone's. Just another senseless death. Probably God trying to kill off everyone he missed with the storm."

They both sat there next to Seth for a while. Erik was still trying to get a handle on what had happened. A few minutes ago, Seth had been smiling, happily petting the horse. It had probably been his best day since finding his family dead the morning after the storm. He'd reminded Erik so much of Sam, with his blonde hair and blue eyes, especially that big smile of his. Now he was dead from a freak, pointless accident.

What in the hell had been the point of Seth even surviving the storm? Erik wondered if maybe he should have left him there, left him sitting on those steps in Hill City. Maybe he'd still be alive.

Tyler found a shovel in the barn. They wrapped Seth in his blanket and buried him with his backpack next to the fence in the pasture. Erik made sure his comic books and *The Lorax* were inside it. He placed the little cobalt-blue Corvette in Seth's hand and closed the boy's fingers around it.

After they were done, as they stood over the grave, neither said anything for a long time. The horse stood patiently by.

"You would have made a great little brother," Erik said, his voice hitching a bit. "I'll miss you, kiddo."

"Goodbye, little dude," Tyler said.

Tyler finished cutting the fence. The horse stopped briefly to sniff at the fresh soil on the grave and then followed them. After about a quarter of a mile, it went off on its own across another field and they never saw it again.

***

They stopped in Bennettville only long enough to pick up some more bottled water and additional food from the local grocery store and so Erik could replace his shirt. He knew by pushing on to Garrison they would probably end up having to sleep outside that night but he didn't care. After Bennettville, they continued trudging along in silence, each keeping to his own thoughts.

As evening neared, they dropped off the side of the road and set up camp along the flat, sandy bank of a creek that had slowed to a mere trickle. Erik started a small campfire and they opened a couple cans of chili they had picked up in town, peeling the labels off and placing them on rocks next to the fire to heat.

Neither had spoken more than a few words each since leaving the pasture that morning. Now, as Tyler reached over to stir his chili, he asked, "Why are we camping off the road? You think there's a danger of a car coming along during the night and running us over?"

Erik shrugged. "Habit, I guess. Mindless adherence to a lifetime of mothers telling us not to play in the street. I don't know. It just feels safer somehow."

Tyler nodded. "Yeah. I've caught myself looking over my shoulder a couple of times to make sure a car isn't coming up behind me. I think of how stupid that is and then twenty minutes later I catch myself doing it again."

"I did that too for a couple of days. Of course, now that I don't look over my shoulder anymore, one of these days some big damn truck will come barreling down the road out of nowhere and turn me into roadkill."

"You think that's possible? You think people can get things working again someday?"

Erik tasted his chili and decided it was hot enough. "I don't know. I guess we'd have to figure out why things don't work in the first place. It might take ten, twenty, a hundred years, but I suppose if enough people survived, someone somewhere is eventually going to figure it out."

They fell into silence again as they ate. Darkness fell around them and the quiet of the night was broken only by the cracks and pops of the campfire.

Finishing his chili, Tyler tossed the can into the campfire. It bounced out and rolled down to the edge of what remained of the creek.

"Something that's been bugging me...," Tyler said, leaning back on his pack. "How did you know his name was Seth?"

Erik stopped midway with his spoon between the can and his mouth. "What?"

"I mean," Tyler continued, "you said that Seth never talked. So how did you know what his name was?"

"It was on his shirt." Erik finished his last bite and tossed his can toward the fire. It missed, bounced, and rolled down next to the one Tyler had tossed. He wiped his mouth with the back of his hand.

"When I found him, he was sitting on the front steps of his house. He didn't respond when I tried to talk to him, so I went into the house to check it out. His mom and dad were dead in the downstairs bedroom. There was a bedroom upstairs with two beds in it. The body of an older boy was in one and the other was empty. I figured the empty one was Seth's. He must have woken up that morning and found his brother dead.

Then he went downstairs and found out his mom and dad were dead too. Poor kid probably freaked out."

"Anyway," he continued, "there was a jersey hanging over the baseboard of the empty bed. You know, like a baseball jersey, except it was probably Little League or Pee Wee. It was on his bed, it was about his size, and it had the name Seth on the back. Plus, it was too small to be his brother's."

Tyler stared at him a minute, a slow grin spreading across his face.

"Are you serious?"

"Yeah. Why?"

"Do you watch sports – baseball, football, basketball?"

"No, I'm not that much into team sports. I watch boxing sometimes."

"Yeah, but you are aware, aren't you, that sports jerseys have the players' *last* names on the back? Not their first."

Erik frowned, considering it. Then the meaning of what Tyler was telling him sank in.

"Shit, you're right. Why in hell didn't I think of that?" He laughed and looked down, shaking his head. "It sounded like a first name, so I guess I just assumed it was." He glanced back up at Tyler, grinning. "So, this whole time I was calling him by his last name."

"Well, he didn't seem to care. I think you probably could have called him Betty and he would have been fine with it."

"Yeah, but damn. I feel like such an idiot now."

"Don't sell yourself short. I'm sure you've been an idiot most of your life."

Movement at the edge of the firelight caught Erik's eye. A young raccoon about the size of a cat waddled out of the darkness. It stopped and studied the two boys, its nose sniffing the air.

"Looks like we have another survivor," Erik said.

"Probably smells the chili."

The raccoon continued along the side of the creek and found the first chili can. The boys watched as it stuck its head into the can and quickly cleaned out every last morsel left inside. After it had cleaned the second can, it glanced at them one last time across the campfire – probably wondering if they had any more – before giving up and continuing its trek along the creek, waddling back into the darkness.

"Well, *that* was exciting," Tyler commented after it was gone.

"I guess that's all we get for entertainment now. Next thing you know, we'll be back to drawing pictures on cave walls with charcoal and colored rocks."

They added more wood to the fire and Erik lay back, staring up at the blackness of the sky. He found his thoughts returning to Seth. He thought of the first night they had spent in Aitkin and how Seth had placed the book in his lap, wanting him to read it aloud, and how many times he had read that same book to his sister. He wondered what his real name had been, but then decided it didn't matter.

To Erik, he would always be Seth, the little boy with the blue eyes and the big smile – the little boy who never spoke a word and never needed to.

JUNE 28

They started out early the next morning. By mid-afternoon, they had passed through the town of Nichols and reached the north shore of Mille Lacs Lake outside of Garrison. They stopped and looked out over the water. With no wind, boats, or even ducks to paddle around on it, the surface of the lake was perfectly flat and smooth, reflecting the dead trees along the shore and the hazy, gray sky above.

"Now that is one flat lake," Tyler commented. "Looks like a giant mirror."

Erik was also admiring the stillness of the lake, and then he began to wonder about something he was not seeing. He studied the surface and then the shore to confirm it.

"There are no fish."

"No what?"

"There are no dead fish. The storm that killed everything else off – people, animals, trees, bugs... Shouldn't this lake be full of dead fish floating around?"

Tyler looked back over the surface of the lake.

"Shit, you're right. This is one of the best lakes for walleye fishing in Minnesota. There should be millions of them floating on the surface."

"Could they all have sunk to the bottom?"

"No. Dead fish float. After a while they might sink but only when they start to rot, or other fish start to eat them."

"Well, then that means the storm must not have killed the fish or anything else under the water. I wonder why not?"

"It's obvious, isn't it?" Tyler said. He paused, for dramatic effect, and then stated, "The fish did it."

"What?"

"Lock two people in a room with a single gun. Open the door later and find only one still alive. It's pretty obvious who the killer is."

Erik hesitated, trying to figure out if Tyler was being serious. "So... you're saying the fish did all this – caused the storm and killed everything on land?"

Tyler nodded to the lake. "There's your proof. Little bastards were probably plotting this for years. Now they can grow legs and take over the world. I think Charles Darwin predicted this a hundred years ago."

Erik stared at him before stating, "You are so full of shit."

Tyler laughed. "Seriously! I bet the first thing they did after the storm was rescue all their little fish brothers and sisters from bowls and aquariums all over the world."

"Yeah, okay," Erik said. "You stay here and bow down to your new fish overlords if you want. I'm going into town to find someplace to stay for tonight. And you know what? I might just find some crackers and a can of tuna for dinner."

Tyler gave him a look of utter horror.

"Blasphemy!"

They followed the highway as it circled around the north end of the lake and into Garrison. There, they passed a trailer park and several small stores and shops before coming to a motel called The Lakeside Inn.

"Wow," Tyler said, staring up at the sign. "I'll bet someone spent a whole day and thirty-two cents coming up with that clever name."

The front door was unlocked and the mummified corpse of a woman was sitting at the front desk, her head down on the guest register as though she had fallen asleep on the job a few hundred years ago. Erik went around to the other side of the desk and looked at the room keys hanging on the wall.

"Get one with two beds," Tyler suggested.

Erik gave him an "are you serious?" look. "You sure you don't want two separate rooms? I might have angered your fish gods. You probably don't want to be in the same room with me when their shock troops arrive and haul me off for re-education."

"Ah, fuck 'em. They're fish. What are they going to do, blow bubbles at us?"

He found a double room with both keys still on the hook. It occurred to him that if this was a more modern motel, with electronic key cards, they would have probably been out of luck.

They found the room and the first thing Erik did was go into the bathroom and try the faucets. There was a slight hiss of air but no water.

"No baths tonight," he announced.

"What the fuck?" Tyler said. "Why wouldn't there be any water? I saw a big-ass water tower when we came into town."

"Once you've gone through a few towns, you'll see that the water supplies can be pretty unreliable. All it takes is one person who was getting a drink of water or running a bath when the storm hit. Just one open faucet will run the water tower dry after a few days."

"Really?"

"Yep. Seth and I were in a town – Hassman, I think it was – and the first house we came to, there was the corpse of a woman in her bathrobe on the kitchen floor. There was a broken glass in the sink and the faucet was turned on. All the water in town had gone right down that one drain. The faucet was even still dripping a little."

"Well, shit," Tyler muttered. "Now I know why you carry water with you everywhere. And here I was thinking it was because you were really thirsty."

They each claimed a bed and then went down the road a short way to a small convenience store and brought back a selection of food and drinks for dinner.

"You realize, don't you," Tyler said, "all this free stuff isn't going to last forever. Sooner or later, it's going to run out and we're going to have to start clubbing our food to death, like those cave men you seem to admire."

"Not a lot left around to club, unless you count a couple of pigeons, a half-starved horse, and a chili-scarfing raccoon. Besides, do we even know how to skin an animal?"

"Ask it nicely to take its fur off?"

"Seriously. It sounds easy enough – shoot an animal for food, like a squirrel, a rabbit, or a deer. But then what? Even if you get its fur off, what then? How do you cut it up?"

"I've seen old movies on TV where they take the rabbit or whatever and run a stick up its ass to roast it over a fire. Seems simple enough, once you remove all the guts and icky stuff."

"Going to be pretty tough roasting an entire deer or cow over a fire."

"My guess is," Tyler said, "that if we're hungry enough, we'll figure it out pretty damn quick."

They ate dinner sitting on their respective beds and talking. They had purposefully brought back cans of tuna and sardines from the store. Once they saw the sardines were whole fish, bones and all, they both stuck to the tuna.

"I suppose," Erik said, "we could probably survive on fish while we figure out the whole hunting thing. At least we know how to do that. And one of the other kids up at that camp showed me how to make a fish trap."

"A fish trap?" Tyler asked, looking dubious. "Did it work?"

"I don't know. That was the night of the storm. I didn't check the trap the next morning. I had other things on my mind."

As evening approached, they lit a lantern and went over Erik's roadmap. Erik was showing Tyler the route he intended to take when a sudden knocking on their door caused them both to freeze and look at each other.

They waited, listening, unsure if what they had heard was real.

Five or six seconds passed and then three more knocks came.

"Hello?" a man's muffled voice called from the other side of the door. "You boys in there?"

Tyler looked at Erik and mouthed, *What the fuck?*

Erik slid off his bed and went to the window. He peeked between the curtains. It was almost full dark outside now. He couldn't see anything, much less anyone standing in front of the door to their room. He turned back to Tyler and gave him a silent shrug.

Three more evenly spaced knocks sounded on the door.

"Come on boys," said the voice. "I know you're in there. I just saw you look out the window. I ain't gonna rape or kill you or nothin'. I'm an old man. I just want to talk."

Now Tyler shrugged.

"Don't look at me. I didn't tell anyone where we were going."

Erik went to the door and opened it slowly, a few inches at first, and looked out. An old man, shorter than Erik and probably about sixty or seventy years old with thinning white hair was standing outside. A scruffy, long-haired, black and brown cat with a white chest and paws darted into the room through the cracked door.

"Don't mind him," the old man chuckled. "He's harmless."

Erik opened the door all the way and the old man entered. He was holding a wine bottle in one hand and a small, unlit lantern in the other.

"Thank you, young man." He placed the lantern on the chair next to the door and held his hand out. "Name's Nils. Saw you two come into town. The missus and I run that trailer park you passed. Well, we used to run it. Ain't been getting' many guests lately."

Erik shook his hand. "I'm Erik. That's Tyler."

Tyler had gotten off the bed and walked over. He shook hands with Nils.

"Is there anyone else in town?"

"Nope, just me and Emma. That's the missus. And the cat there." The cat was doing circles around Tyler's legs. "Don't know his name. Showed up 'bout a week ago. I made the mistake of feeding him 'cause he was so damned skinny. Now he follows me around everywhere." He held the bottle up. "You boys like brandy?"

Erik shrugged. "Never had it before."

"Me neither," Tyler said. He had knelt to one knee and was petting the cat. The cat continued circling and rubbing on his legs, purring loudly.

"It's peach brandy. One of our guests, Jack, comes up from Florida every summer and stays in that ugly silver and red trailer parked near the back. He makes it himself and brings me a bottle every time he comes up." Nils shrugged. "I don't drink much myself anymore, so I've got a little stockpile of it."

Erik unwrapped the plastic motel room cups that were on the desk and Nils filled each with about an inch of the light-colored alcohol. He handed one each to Erik and Tyler and lifted his own.

"*Prost!*" Tyler announced.

Nils hesitated, looking either surprised or amused. "*Zum Wohl!*" he replied.

Erik wasn't sure what they were saying but he raised his cup and drank with them. It tasted like peach-flavored cough syrup with a kick.

"You speak German?" Nils asked Tyler.

"My grandfather on my mother's side taught me a little. He was an old German who liked to drink. I don't remember much of it, but what I do is mostly related to drinking and swearing."

Nils laughed. "That's what us old Germans are best at."

He refilled their cups and they drank and talked for a while. Tyler placed the open sardine cans on the floor and the cat attacked the oily fish with starving feline ferocity.

They learned that Nils was a cop from Chicago who was forced to retire fifteen years ago after taking two bullets to the chest during a drug raid. His wife also retired from her job as a parole officer and they had bought the trailer park so they could spend their remaining years away from the gangs, drugs, and guns of the city streets.

"I bet you don't have much trouble from your guests," Tyler said.

"They're mostly all old and retired too. The young folks, they stay in the cabins farther down the lake where they can get their satellite TV and plug their gadgets into the internet."

The boys gave him a summary of their travels so far, starting with what Erik had seen the night of the storm and ending with their arrival here on their way to Iowa.

"I'm truly sorry about your friend," Nils said, shaking his head after they told him about Seth. "That must have been tough. But you boys, you need to be extra careful from now on. And I ain't talking about accidents."

"What do you mean?" Erik asked.

"I'm talking about other people, like that crazy guy you told me about, the one you had to put out of his misery. If you're going all the way to

Iowa, you're likely to run across more people who survived that storm of yours. And they're not all going to be friendly old Germans like me or crazy drug users content with blowing things up. As an old cop, I can tell you there are people out there who will want to hurt you purely for their own enjoyment. And with no rules or laws anymore, they're gonna be twice as dangerous."

"So, you think we should avoid people altogether?" Tyler asked.

"No, not necessarily. But you need to be smart. And alert. Always be aware of your surroundings. Notice things. If anyone or anything seems a bit off to you, avoid it. Learn to trust your gut. It'll save your life." He looked back and forth between them. "Either of you boys carryin' a gun?"

Erik and Tyler glanced at each other and then both shook their heads.

"What about the gun you used for that mercy killing?"

"I left it there," Erik said. "It was pretty burned up and had only one bullet left in it."

Nils thought for a bit, nodding. "I think I can help you out there. But for now…" He stood and stretched his back. "I should be gettin' back to the wife. She's not well and she's been getting worse. You boys stop by before you leave tomorrow morning. It's the little house sitting there by the road that leads into the trailer park – has a little sign that says Office above the door. Emma will be glad to see you."

They followed Nils and his cat to the door. The old man dug a small box of wooden matches out of his pocket, struck one, and transferred the flame to his lantern. It was full dark now. He stepped outside and then turned back to them.

"One last bit of advice. Step out here a minute."

Erik and Tyler stepped outside. Nils pointed to the window of their room. The light from their lantern inside was clearly visible around the edges of the curtains.

"You can see light like that a mile away," Nils said, "maybe more in this darkness. You'll want to keep that in mind. You don't want to be advertising your presence to the wrong sort of people." He nodded to them and said "Good night" before turning and heading back up the road toward the trailer park. The nameless cat trotted along behind him.

JUNE 29

Tyler removed the note taped to the door of the office and read it. "Well, shit." He handed the note to Erik.

>Boys,
>I'm sorry, but I won't be able to see you off in the morning. Emma took a turn for the worse after I got home from visiting you and passed away during the night. I'm too old to face this strange new world without her so I've chosen to join her wherever she's gone.
>I've left you a couple of my old service pistols and plenty of ammunition to practice with. I hope you never have to use them but, if you do, do so without hesitation. If you're in a bad situation, don't hope it will go away, because it won't. Make it go away.
>Good luck on your journey. Stay alert, stay safe, and stay alive. I hope everything goes well and you find what you're looking for.
>And if you see the cat before you leave, give him a scratch between the ears. He likes that.
>Gute reise, meine freunde,
>Nils

Erik read the note twice. "Damn. I liked him." He glanced to Tyler. "What does that mean at the end?"

"Good journey, my friends."

Erik thought about it. "It doesn't sound plural."

"The E at the ends of *meine* and *freunde* make it plural. Don't think about it too much. It's German. It's weird."

Erik folded the note and put it in his pocket. On the doorstep was a cloth-wrapped bundle, a bottle of the same peach brandy they had drank last night, and a can of cat food sitting in a small, wooden bowl. He unwrapped the bundle. Inside were two pistols and four boxes of bullets. He picked one of the guns up and looked it over. It was a sleek, chrome pistol with a black handle.

"Smith and Wesson forty-five ACP." He held it out to Tyler.

Tyler shook his head. "Like I said before, I don't know anything about pistols. I'd probably end up shooting my foot off."

"You just need lessons. This is the safety." Erik pointed to a lever on the side of the pistol. "Make sure that's on before you load, carry, or unload the gun. Only take it off to shoot." He pressed a button on the side with his thumb and the clip dropped from the handle. "This is your clip. It holds ten shots. Looks like we're fully loaded. If you want, you can put an additional round in the chamber for eleven. Slap it back in to make sure it's tight." He slapped the clip back into the handle.

"Pull the top slide back," he continued, "to load the first bullet into the chamber unless you already have one loaded." He pulled the slide back and let it snap forward again. "When the slide goes back, it cocks the hammer here. See? Now you're ready to party. It's an automatic, which means it's self-loading and self-cocking after the first shot. It will fire as fast as you can pull the trigger. When you're out of bullets the slide will lock back. You drop the clip, reload it or put a fresh one in, and press right here to let the slide go forward again. Now you're ready for round two."

He put his thumb on the hammer, pulled the trigger, and gently eased the hammer forward to uncock it. He held the pistol out to Tyler again.

Tyler took the pistol, keeping a wary eye on Erik.

"You're scary sometimes, you know that?"

"Cop's kid, remember? Mom and Dad were separated but he came around about every weekend or so. His idea of a day out with his son was a day at the shooting range."

Tyler looked at the pistol. "It's on safety now, right?"

"Yep. Don't worry. We'll do some target shooting later. You need to get familiar with it is all."

Tyler glanced at the second pistol still lying in the bundle on the doorstep.

"What's that one?"

Erik picked it up. "Ruger Blackhawk forty-four-magnum revolver." He looked at the bullets in the cylinder. "Wadcutters. Damn! These will do some damage."

"Is it powerful?"

"Ever see the movie *Dirty Harry*, where he talks about the most powerful handgun in the world?" He held the revolver up. "This is it, though he used an automatic version. There's a reason they call it a hand-cannon. And it's loaded with wadcutters. They have a flat front and are usually used for target practice. But if you shoot someone with these, it won't matter where you hit them. These things blow body parts off."

"Sounds like the perfect gun for you. I'll stick with the pretty one."

Erik handed Tyler two boxes of bullets for the forty-five. He put the forty-four and the other two boxes of bullets into his own backpack along with the bottle of brandy. He glanced around.

"See the cat anywhere?"

Tyler also looked around. "Nope."

Erik opened the can of cat food and dumped it into the bowl.

"Well, if he comes back, at least he'll have one last good meal before he has to start hunting mice and birds again."

"Not that there are any around," Tyler added. "He'd better be a damn good hunter or learn to fish. Either that or go vegan."

"Vegan? Isn't that like vegetarian?"

"Yep. It's an old Indian word. Means lousy hunter."

They left the trailer park and continued around the west side of the lake. It took the better part of the day before they reached the south end. There was a small cluster of cabins along the shoreline. They picked a cabin at random and quickly confirmed it had not been occupied the night of the storm.

After dropping their backpacks off in the cabin, they took their newly acquired pistols and ammunition next door, where Erik proceeded to give Tyler gun handling and shooting lessons. He had Tyler practice loading and unloading the pistol and then taught him how to aim and shoot. They used the door and windows of the next cabin as targets.

"Use your fingertip on the trigger," Erik advised him. "Squeeze it straight back. Don't jerk it. And don't anticipate the recoil. Each shot should come as a surprise."

After several shots, Tyler was able to hit the windows in the next cabin with an ease and accuracy that surprised Erik.

"You're a natural. Just remember, don't be in a hurry and never, ever shoot from the hip or hold the gun sideways like they do in the movies. If you do, you'll never hit your target. Take a breath, aim, fire, repeat. Make Wyatt Earp proud."

"What about you? I want to see what that hand-cannon can do."

Erik looked around and picked out a mailbox about thirty feet away. He cocked the revolver, set his feet apart, and took aim using a two-handed grip. He pulled the trigger. The recoil of the pistol jerked his arms up over his head. The explosive sound of the gunshot was deafening. The mailbox flew off its post.

"*Jesus Christ!*" Tyler shouted, jumping back and covering his ears too late. He shook his head and tried to use his fingertips to pop his ears. "Holy shit. That thing is fucking *loud.*"

Erik laughed, though his own ears were ringing and he could barely hear what Tyler was saying.

"That's why it's called a hand-cannon."

"Fucking warn me next time. Jesus! Are my ears bleeding?"

They walked down the lane and examined the mailbox. There was a small hole about the size of a nickel in one side. On the opposite side, the steel was pealed back in jagged petals around a hole the size of a half-dollar.

"Damn," Tyler breathed, examining the exit hole. "I see what you mean. That thing does do some major damage."

They reloaded their pistols and went back to the cabin. It was a rental so there was no food or supplies worth scavenging from the cupboards. Tyler, however, did find a Bowie knife and leather sheath that had slipped down and been lost behind a clothes dresser. The blade was at least twelve inches long and almost two inches wide. He tested the sharpness of the blade on the edge of the table and then slid it back into its sheath.

"What are you going to use that for?" Erik asked. "Do you think we might run across a bear or moose we might have to skin?"

"You never know," Tyler replied, attaching the knife and sheath to his belt. "If we run across a moose, you can shoot it with your hand-cannon and I'll skin what's left with my big damn knife."

JULY 5

They continued south on 169 for the next six days, passing through small towns, sleeping indoors when they could, and seeing scattered signs of life along the way. A mile outside of Vineland, they saw an owl sitting in a tree at the edge of the woods. Later, they passed a field with about thirty dead cows and one still alive. In Onima, they came across a skittish black and white dog that darted between a couple of houses ahead of them. Every so often, they would see an occasional sparrow, crow, or other type of bird. But, like the squirrels and farm animals, even the birds were few and far between.

On the afternoon of the sixth day after leaving Garrison, they were passing a ranch-style house on a small acreage off the highway south of Milaca when Tyler talked Erik into calling it quits early, at least two hours before darkness.

"We've been pushing it pretty hard," he said. "If I don't get a couple extra hours of sleep tonight, you're going to be dragging my sorry ass down this highway tomorrow morning."

Erik had gotten out of the habit of knocking before entering houses. They had found not one house this whole time with a living occupant in it. And, as it turned out, they didn't even have to force their way into this one. The front door was unlocked.

"Country folks," Tyler said. "My grandfather never locked his door, either. Of course, he did have a big goddamn Irish wolfhound that liked to sleep on the couch. That dog was the size of a small horse and must have weighed a hundred-fifty pounds. Don't think there's a burglar alive that would want to tackle something like that."

"I thought wolfhounds were supposed to be smart and friendly."

"They are, but a grizzly bear can look friendly and playful too, right up until it decides to eat you."

While Erik immediately went to the kitchen to forage for supplies, Tyler decided it might be nice to sit on an actual toilet for once instead of squatting in the woods or in a ditch at the side of the road.

Erik was surprised at how little there was in the cupboards and pantry. As he was sorting through boxes of macaroni and cans of tomato sauce and mushrooms in the narrow space, a shadow fell over him. He straightened and turned just as a carving knife sliced past his shoulder and buried itself into one of the pantry shelves.

"Jesus!"

On defensive instinct, he shoved the old woman in the nightgown back against the pantry door and quickly twisted his way out of the small room, backpedaling into the kitchen.

The woman's screams were all fury and pure rage. She came after Erik, reaching for him with dirty fingers that curved like claws. What frightened Erik the most was neither her savage screams nor her sudden attack but her appearance. She looked like any of the hundreds of mummies he'd seen since the storm – sunken eyes, leathery skin, and a death-grin made worse by the horrific sounds she was making.

She was a living corpse. She shouldn't have been alive but she was.

The woman lunged at him, her clawed hands going for his face. Erik screamed, batted her hands away, turned, and ran from the kitchen. He was half-way to the front door when he remembered Tyler.

"Tyler!" he shouted. "Get out of the house. Now!"

He skidded to a stop on the front porch and looked back. The woman was not following him.

"Shit!"

He looked around quickly for a board or stick or anything else he could use as a weapon.

Another horrendous shriek came from inside the house. Damn. Did she have Tyler trapped?

"Goddammit," he muttered. He quickly shrugged off his pack and ran back inside the house, almost colliding with Tyler in the entryway.

"Jesus, get out of here!" Tyler shouted, pushing past him.

The screeching woman was stumbling out of the hallway, clawing at the air, the walls, anything she could reach.

"No shit," Erik muttered. He sprinted after Tyler, slamming the door closed behind him to slow the woman and grabbing his backpack as he jumped from the porch.

They ran as fast as they could to the highway before stopping and turning back to the house. Out of breath, they both stood on the highway, leaning forward with their hands on their knees, gasping for air and hearts pounding while they watched the front door. After several minutes, they looked at each other and both burst out with nervous, relieved laughter.

"Jesus Christ," Tyler said. "What in the hell was that thing?"

"I think that was our first zombie," Erik said. "She almost got me with a knife."

"She almost got *me* on the shitter. If you hadn't shouted when you did..."

They stood for another minute or two, watching the house. The door remained closed and the shrieking had stopped.

"Still tired?" Erik asked.

"Fuck. I don't think I'll be able to sleep for a week after that."

They adjusted their packs and resumed their trek down the highway. Every so often, one or both of them would cast a quick glance behind, just to make sure.

"So, what did we learn back there?" Tyler asked after they'd put almost a mile between themselves and the house.

"Don't get caught with your pants down?" Erik asked, grinning at him.

"How about always fucking knock first," Tyler said.

"Yeah, that works too."

***

That night they camped by the side of the road. Before the light of the day failed completely, Erik checked his map and saw they had another thirty or so miles to go before they reached the next town.

They had passed another field full of dead cows and a pasture with half a dozen dead horses and two live ones. Rather than cut the fence wire again, they simply opened the gate and then continued on their way, leaving the horses to figure it out for themselves.

By Erik's estimate, the number of animal corpses they passed outnumbered live animals by nearly a thousand to one. He figured the same ratio probably held true for trees and humans as well.

"Pretty unbiased storm," he noted. "Killed everything in equal measure."

"Except the fucking fish," Tyler replied. "Slimy little bastards anyway."

The weather had not changed much. There was still no breeze and the sky was still overcast with the same hazy, uniform shade of gray. But the temperature was beginning to drop little by little. Erik was beginning to feel it, especially at night when it could get downright chilly. In the town of Milaca, before the ranch house, they had picked up a couple of extra shirts and light jackets. They had also swapped out their blankets for insulated sleeping bags.

"Looks like another five or six days before we hit Elk River," Erik said, folding his map and returning it to the side pocket of his backpack.

"Elk River's pretty big," Tyler said. He had started the campfire tonight and was poking at it with a long stick. "If you're one-in-a-thousand theory is correct, there's probably a few people still alive there." He sat back and blew on the burning point of his stick. "Plus, when you go from Elk River to Minneapolis, you pass through a bunch of smaller towns, but it's really just one big suburb of Minneapolis. You can't tell when you're leaving one town and entering another unless you pay attention to the signs."

Erik stared at the fire, thinking.

"If there are enough survivors there," he said, "they might have found each other by now and started getting serious about survival. It's been what, three weeks since the storm? Maybe four?"

"Don't have a clue." Tyler tossed his stick into the fire. "Shit, I think calendars are pretty much obsolete now anyway. I don't even know what month it is. Are we still in June?"

"I don't know. I could probably figure it out if I sat down with a pencil and backtracked each day on the map, but what's the point?" He picked up a stick of his own and stirred the fire a bit.

"So, if we do come across some small community of survivors, are you going to stay with them?" he asked.

Tyler leaned back on his backpack with his arms folded across his chest and stared up at the starless night sky.

"Yeah, I did say that, didn't I?" He paused, thinking. "I don't know. I guess it all depends. I mean, if it's a bunch of guys or old people, I don't think I'd fit in. But if there's, you know, a couple of hot chicks, then I'd have to seriously consider dumping your ass."

"That would be tempting," Erik agreed. "But if there are more guys than girls, you're going to have some competition."

"Competition? Ha! I'm young, handsome, and in the prime of life. If you're looking to restart the human race, take a number, ladies, and I'll get back to you."

Erik laughed and shook his head. "I don't think a line like that is going to work on too many girls, even at the end of the world."

"Well, what line would you use?"

"I wouldn't use a line at all. Just be yourself, man." He thought about that for a moment. "On second thought, maybe that's a bad idea. You're kind of like the boorish, crude uncle no one wants to invite to Thanksgiving dinner. Maybe you *should* come up with a good line."

"Fuck you. How many girls have *you* scored with?"

Erik hesitated, considered a lie, and then decided against it. It was the end of the world, after all.

"None. I have – *had* – a couple of friends who were girls but no actual girlfriends. Shit, I'm fifteen and from a small town in the middle of nowhere. What do you want?"

"Have you ever even kissed a girl?"

"Not that it makes any difference now but, yes, I have."

"Mothers and sisters don't count, choir boy. No relatives, even if she's your cousin and you're from Tennessee."

"It was back in first grade. We didn't know what we were doing. I think we were mostly pretending we were boyfriend-girlfriend. Somehow, we ended up in the teacher's coat closet. I don't remember who started it but, hey, we gave it a shot."

"In first grade?" Tyler looked impressed. "Making out in the teacher's coat closet? You hound dog! I bet you still remember her name."

Erik had to smile, because Tyler was right.

"Natalie. She moved away the next year. I never heard where she went. But since then, I've been too busy taking care of my sister and all. With Mom and Dad separated, I don't have much time to be chasing girls." He leaned back on his rolled up sleeping bag and stared at the fire for a while before asking, "So what about you? Are you some Casanova or are you full of shit?"

"I'm full of shit," Tyler admitted. "I didn't kiss a girl until last year. It was at a school basketball game. I was sitting there on the bleachers, watching our team suck again, when this girl I kind of liked and a couple of her friends came and sat down beside me. They were chit-chatting and I don't think they even noticed me sitting there. Anyway, I'd always kind of had the hots for her and there weren't that many people at the game. At some point, she turned back to the game, watched it for a minute, and then turned in my direction." He held his hand up, palm out. "God as my witness, I don't know why, but that's when I planted one right smack on her lips."

Erik grinned. "You masher."

Tyler gave a resigned sigh. "She kissed me back at first, and then I think she suddenly realized what she was doing. She pulled back with this look of shock and anger in her eyes and hauled off and smacked me right across the face. Her and her friends got up and stormed off." He paused again. Erik could tell this was the first and probably last time he was ever going to tell this story to anyone.

Tyler shook his head, staring at the fire. "I saw her in the hallway a few times after that but she never, ever looked at me again. And I never tried to talk to her, even to apologize. I felt like such a jackass."

"Whatever happened to her?"

"I saw less and less of her. She was two grades ahead of me, so we weren't even in the same classes."

Now it was Erik's turn to be impressed.

"She was that much older than you, and you up and went for it on a whim? Man, you've got some balls."

Tyler grinned. "I think she would have cut them off if she'd had a knife. She was really, *really* pissed off."

They talked for a while longer and were starting to roll their sleeping bags out when they heard crunching in the dry grass beyond the light of the campfire. They both froze. Erik thought of the revolver in his backpack. Why in hell was it in his backpack where he couldn't get to it quickly? He could imagine Nils shaking his head sadly at such a stupid mistake.

A deer stepped into the firelight. It was a small buck with velvet still on its antlers. It stopped and turned its head left and then right, its ears up and alert. Its eyes were milky white and Erik guessed it was blind. It must have followed the sound of their voices.

"Looks like it's sick," Tyler whispered.

The deer turned its head to the sound of his voice. Large patches of fur were missing all over its body, exposing dry, leathery skin.

"Weird," Erik whispered back. "It's like it's half-mummified but still alive, like that old woman back there. Must be an after-effect of the storm."

The deer turned its head again and stomped its hoof. It was nervous and getting ready to run, but it was facing the campfire.

Erik guessed the deer didn't know the fire was there. It couldn't see it. He wondered if it could even smell the smoke or feel the heat.

"Hey!" he shouted suddenly, clapping his hands at the same time.

The deer wheeled away from them and the fire and bounded back off into the darkness from the direction it had come. Erik could hear it crashing through the brush and trees. He wondered how long its luck would hold out before it ran smack into a tree or broke its leg tripping over something. But it had lasted this long, hadn't it?

Tyler looked at him, one eyebrow raised.

"Damn thing was about to step into the fire," Erik explained.

Tyler seemed to consider it but didn't reply. He went back to spreading his sleeping bag out.

"Besides," Erik continued, "would you have wanted to eat it? It was sick. How do you know it wasn't contagious or something?"

"I didn't say anything," Tyler said, crawling into his sleeping bag. "But you're right. It probably wouldn't have been a good idea."

Erik crawled into his own sleeping bag and stared up at the black sky. As Tyler had said back in Garrison, the free food and supplies wouldn't last forever, especially not if they started finding other survivors. The day was coming when they would have to start shooting or trapping their food – sick, blind, or otherwise.

JULY 9

"Looks like we missed the big going-out-of-business sale," Tyler said as he and Erik walked among the bare shelves, broken display cases, and empty gun racks of the sporting goods store. He kicked aside an empty Red Ryder box. "Hell, they even took the damn BB guns."

"Would have taken a small army to cart all this stuff off," Erik said. "Or one very determined hoarder."

"Probably some damn survivalist nuts. Who else would take everything? Even the BB guns for God's sake. It's the end of the world. What in the hell would anyone need a dozen BB guns for?"

"Maybe it was a troop of Cub Scouts."

They searched through what remained in the store – some clothing, mosquito spray, boating supplies… but found nothing they either wanted or needed. They returned to the front of the store, where the steel bars on the outer security door had been twisted and wrenched from their frame. The heavy, wooden inner door had been battered down with an ax.

Outside in the parking lot, Erik looked around, considering their next move.

The sporting goods store was in a strip mall off the highway in Elk River. He had hoped to replenish their supply of ammunition for their pistols. They had been target shooting off and on since leaving Garrison ten days ago and were down to only five or six bullets apiece.

"So, what now, oh great white leader of the apocalypse?" Tyler asked.

"Which way do you suppose they went?"

"Who? The gun thieves? Why? You thinking of reasoning with them? Do you think if we ask real nice, they'll bring all the stuff back?"

"No, I'm thinking more like, if they went this way, then we should go that way."

"Sorry," Tyler said. "I left my Davy Crockett tracking book back at my place."

Erik glanced up at the overcast sky and located the dim spot of the sun. It was mid-afternoon.

"We probably have four or five hours before dark. Maybe we should keep going for another couple of hours and then find a place to crash for the night."

"Might want to get off the highway too," Tyler added. "If we do have some survivalist nuts running around with a few hundred guns, making ourselves targets on a deserted road probably isn't the smartest thing to do."

Erik had to admit that Tyler had a point. He thought of what Nils had said to them.

There are people out there who will want to hurt you purely for their own enjoyment. And with no rules or laws anymore, they're going to be twice as dangerous.

Two teenage boys walking down the middle of a deserted highway would certainly make easy targets.

Instead of returning to the highway, they crossed over to the bypass road that ran parallel to it and then followed the bypass for a short way until it crossed a boulevard that headed west through a residential area. A median lined with large oak and ash trees ran down the center of the boulevard. The houses on either side were older, two-story homes of brick and wood set back on spacious front lawns.

They walked up one side of the boulevard, keeping to the sidewalk instead of their usual middle-of-the-street approach. Erik didn't know if it would make them any safer if someone decided to start taking pot-shots at them, but at least they were less exposed and closer to the houses if they suddenly needed to run for cover.

He casually glanced at the houses as they passed each one, first looking for a likely place to spend the night and then with a growing feeling of unease at what he was seeing. He stopped and stared up one side of the boulevard and then the other, scanning the windows, looking for the shift of a curtain, a twitch of a blind, or the fleeting shadow of someone suddenly ducking out of sight.

Tyler had also noticed the markings. He came up beside Erik and glanced slowly around.

"Okay, what's with all the creepy crosses?"

On every house on either side of the street, a large, bright red cross had been sloppily painted on the front door.

"I don't know," Erik said, still studying the windows. "But I don't like it. I don't see anyone but that doesn't mean we're not being watched."

Now Tyler also looked at the windows.

"We should probably get off the street."

"Go forward? Or back?"

"Maybe go into one of these houses. Hang out 'til morning and then get the hell out of Dodge."

Erik agreed. The sooner they got off the street, the better.

They went up the steps of the nearest house. Erik noted the splintered wood of the door jamb next to the lock and pointed it out to Tyler.

"Someone's already been in here."

Tyler shrugged his backpack off. "Fuck this." He dug his pistol out. Erik did the same.

Holding their pistols at the ready, they took positions on either side of the cross-marked door. Erik used his foot to push it the rest of the way open. He waited to a count of three and then cautiously peered inside.

The interior of the house was dim and shadowy. He let his gaze move slowly over everything he could see – several pairs of shoes on the floor of the entryway, a short bench, an empty coat rack along the wall. Beyond this, he could see a couch and a recliner in the adjacent living room. There were two more rooms to the left and one to the right but he couldn't see all the way into them. Nothing moved or looked out of the ordinary.

He glanced back to Tyler and gave a slight shrug. "Looks empty." He then turned and stepped carefully into the entryway.

Tyler followed and they walked slowly through the house, being as quiet as they could. They moved from the entryway to the living room, checking out a sitting room and some kind of study or home office and kitchen along the way. It looked like every other house Erik had been in since the storm, as though someone still lived here but had stepped out for a minute. The only thing that broke the illusion was the absolute silence in the house – the feeling that it was abandoned.

There was a master bedroom on the first floor. The blankets had been stripped from the mattress. They lay with the pillows in a pile at the foot of the bed. The sheets had also been stripped from the bed but there was no sign of them. Also missing was any sign of the previous occupants.

"Better check upstairs," Erik said.

There were two more bedrooms upstairs. The first was the room of a pre-teen girl, with animal posters, stuffed animals, and a child-size dresser, desk, and vanity. The second bedroom belonged to a teenage boy and was dominated by a large desk holding a computer, two big-screen monitors, speakers, a gaming console, and several dozen computer game boxes. Like in the master bedroom, both kids' beds had been stripped down to the bare mattresses. Sheets and bodies alike were also missing.

"Probably," Tyler suggested, "someone was still alive and buried the bodies, like I did with my parents. I wrapped them in sheets and blankets too."

"Makes sense. But what's with the crosses on all the doors? And if someone in this house survived long enough to bury the others, why was the door forced open?"

"Crosses are probably just some religious nut – thinks he's keeping vampires away or the dead from rising. And, hell, you've been forcing doors open all up and down the state, staying in houses and raiding kitchens. You don't think anyone else has figured out that little survival hack?"

"Okay," Erik said, "maybe you're right. But it seems a little odd that we'd find all three in a single house."

"We can go check a couple of other houses if you really have your heart all set on playing Scooby Doo."

Erik considered it and then shook his head. "Screw it. Let's crash here tonight and get back on the road tomorrow. We'll restock what we can and keep an eye out for other stores that might have ammunition."

"We should start checking the houses too. Lots of people own guns, you know."

Erik hadn't even considered that. Of course. He'd heard once that American citizens owned more guns than all the world's armies combined. Chances were they'd already stayed at a dozen houses with guns and ammunition in them.

They made a quick search of the house but found only a BB gun and a twenty-two caliber rifle with half a box of shells. Neither of them felt like toting a rifle around. They did, however, agree that a rifle would eventually become a necessity when they had to start hunting for their food.

They moved a couch from the living room to brace the front door for the night, closed all the curtains, and kept their use of lantern light to a bare minimum. The possible presence of survivalists or whoever had raided the sporting goods store didn't worry Erik that much. Survivalists would probably be arrogant and self-assured, walking in the open with their guns in plain sight. He figured they would be able to spot any survivalists long before they were spotted themselves and have time to hide.

Whoever had painted the crosses on the doors, however, did worry him. The crosses implied religion. And die-hard believers in divine judgment would be dangerous in any apocalypse.

JULY 10

Instead of immediately returning to the highway the next morning and leaving town, they decided to continue east along the boulevard and then cut across to an older part of town. To the best of Tyler's memory, having been to Elk River several times before, there was another sporting goods store somewhere around there.

The crosses on the doors continued to appear all the way down the boulevard. Out of curiosity, they investigated one house where the front door was not only marked but also wide open. They confirmed that not only had the door been forced, but that the bedrooms in this house were also lacking in mummified corpses and sheets.

Checking a second and then a third, fourth, and fifth house led to the same results. A small, two-story brick house near the end of the boulevard, however, stood out from the rest. Its door had also been forced but had no cross painted on it.

They encountered the body of the occupant as soon as they entered the house. It was that of a man, probably in his early forties, but he hadn't been mummified by the storm. Instead, he had hung himself with a garden hose from the upstairs banister. It looked as though he'd been dead for more than a week.

There was a note written on yellow, legal paper and pinned to his chest:

> Devoted my whole life to my family, my church, and my god. This is the reward I receive. Screw all this. We are forsaken.

Family pictures in the living room and master bedroom indicated there should have been three more bodies in the house – his wife and two daughters. But their corpses were missing, as well as the sheets from their beds.

"Wonder why they didn't cut him down and take him too," Erik said after they'd returned from the bedrooms and were staring up at the hanged man again.

"Maybe because he's a suicide," Tyler suggested. "Might be they only take people killed by the storm."

"Yeah, but why?"

"Because mummies make better jerky?"

Tyler's humor sometimes made Erik's stomach lurch a bit.

They left the man hanging and closed the door behind them.

"I'm thinking every house on this street is like this," Erik said. "Someone has been through here clearing out all of the mummified corpses, all of the storm victims."

"Must be more than one person doing it. If they're burying them, can you imagine a single person digging that many graves?"

Curious, they checked the backyard of the house. There was a gardening shed and charcoal grill, a small dog kennel holding the mummified corpse of a bulldog, a swing set, a playhouse, and a trampoline, but there was no sign of a grave. Looking into the backyards of the neighboring houses, they could see no signs of fresh digging in those yards, either.

"So, now we've got the mystery of the missing mummies," Tyler said. "Do we want to go all Scooby Doo on this or do we want to find that gun store and get the hell out of town?"

"I say let Scooby Doo and the gang handle this one. I don't think I want to know what someone is doing with a few hundred dried-up corpses."

"Yeah," Tyler agreed. "And if we meet some kindly old lady who invites us in for a nice, hot bowl of stew, maybe we ought to politely decline."

The returned to the boulevard and continued to the end where they turned south again onto a cross-street. This led them to a small business district that looked older than the rest of the town.

The gun store Tyler remembered was a small brick building on the corner. It had been broken into like the sporting goods store in the strip mall. And, like the one in the strip mall, it had been completely cleaned out.

"Well, this was a complete waste of time," Erik said, disappointed. "I think we're going to have to go with your suggestion and start checking every house we stay in."

"Makes me wonder," Tyler said. "Is this the same group that's taking the bodies out of the houses?"

"Or are there two groups? One hoarding guns and ammo and the other hoarding corpses."

Tyler shook his head. "You know what? I don't even want to know. There's something weird going on around here and I think we've spent just about enough time in this creepy little berg."

They continued through the older section of town and then headed east to link up with highway 169 again. The houses along this street also had red crosses painted on their front doors. As the street began to curve to the south again, they decided to cut straight west through the yards in order to save time and a couple of miles. They moved between houses and climbed over a low backyard fence, finding themselves at the edge of a wide-open, grassy field.

At the other end of the field was a white, modern-style church setting atop a long, low, treeless hill. The church was single-story with stained-glass windows, a steel roof, and an incredibly narrow steel spire rising to a sharp point about forty feet into the air. But it was the hillside below the church that caused them both to stop and stare.

Lined up in several ruler-straight rows all along the hill were what at first glance could have been mistaken for giant cocoons. Most were white but some were pale blue, light green, or another color. And although most were from five to six feet long, a few were considerably smaller.

"Those aren't what I think they are, are they?" Tyler asked.

"I'm pretty sure they are," Erik replied grimly.

He did a quick count in his head. He estimated there were over two hundred corpses lined in rows along the hillside, each tightly wrapped in its own bedsheet.

"Well, that solves the mystery of the missing mummies," Tyler said. "And we didn't even need those meddling kids or their stupid, talking dog."

"Must be some survivors using the church," Erik said. "But why not bury the bodies? Why take them out of the houses and then line them all up in rows on a hill?"

Before Tyler could reply, the doors to the church opened and a fat, bearded man wearing jeans with suspenders, a flannel shirt, and a dirty baseball cap stepped out. He carried a hunting rifle with an attached scope slung over one shoulder and at least three pistols tucked under a belt around his expansive waist. A pair of binoculars hung from a lanyard around his thick neck.

"Rut row," Tyler said in a dead-on Scooby Doo imitation.

"Shit! Hide."

They quickly scooted behind a small line of bushes to their left and crouched as low as they could while still being able to look out across the field to the church.

"Why is it that all psycho survivors wear suspenders?" Tyler whispered. "Is that written down in a handbook somewhere?"

The fat man stepped out of the doorway and looked out over the grassy field below. He lifted the binoculars to his eyes and scanned all along the edge of the field from left to right. He paused when he reached the stretch of bushes the boys were hiding behind and gave it extra scrutiny. Erik and Tyler lay as flat and still as they could, neither daring to even breathe until the man's gaze moved from them and he continued scanning elsewhere.

"What's he up to?" Erik whispered.

"I think we're about to find out," Tyler whispered back.

The fat man, finished with scanning the field, turned back to the church and opened the door again. But instead of going in, he stood to the side and held the door open. A few seconds later, a tall, thin woman with long red hair stepped out of the church. She was wearing a white robe with gold trim that went all the way to her sandal-clad feet. She walked carefully, purposefully, like she was leading a solemn procession. She held an oversized bible clutched tightly against her breasts.

Two more women followed behind her. The older one was a heavy-set brunette. The other was a smaller, younger woman with dirty-blonde hair. They wore identical plain red robes with sandals and carried a makeshift stretcher between them. On the stretcher was one of the sheet-wrapped, mummified corpses apparently taken from one of the houses.

Following the two women with the stretcher, five more women in red robes and sandals also exited the church.

"Ah, the plot thickens…," Tyler whispered ominously.

The tall, bible-toting woman led the two stretcher-bearers down the hill to the end of the last row of corpses. The other five stayed at the top of the hill, spacing themselves out in a line and bowing their heads. They pressed their hands together in front of them as if in prayer.

The fat man let the church door swing closed and stood looking out over the field, casually glancing left and then right. He seemed to have no interest in what the women were doing.

Stopping at the end of the row, the tall woman held out one hand, palm up, indicating to the other two where they should lay the body. Once the two women had lined up the body but before they laid it down, the redhead carefully knelt in the grass and bowed her head.

The two women lowered the corpse to the ground. The lifted it from the stretcher and then positioned it so that its head lay upon the redhead's lap. They then knelt on either side of the corpse and placed their hands on it, bowing their own heads.

After a few seconds in which she could have been praying, the tall woman raised her head and tilted her face to the sky. Still with her eyes closed, she began speaking. She was too far away for Erik to hear her words but it sounded like she was chanting the same phrase over and over again in a rhythmic, monotone voice.

"Oh man, this is getting creepy," Tyler said. "If that fucking corpse suddenly sits up…"

The chanting continued for a full minute. When she was done, the woman again bowed her head for a few seconds. Her two helpers gently lifted the corpse's head from her lap so she could stand and then lowered it to the ground again before also standing. The redhead then led them back up the hill to the church. The five other women fell into step behind them.

The fat man pulled the door open and held it until all the women were inside. He followed them and let the door close behind him.

The boys waited a couple of minutes to make sure the church door didn't open again.

"What in the hell was that all about?" Erik asked.

"Some kind of creepy-ass séance," Tyler replied, "complete with armed, hillbilly bodyguard. I don't know about you but that was a little too cult-like for me."

"Me too. Let's get out of here."

Keeping low, they backed away from the bushes until they reached the fence again. They jumped the fence and returned to the street, once more heading south but still needing to reconnect with the highway.

"Make a note," Erik said. "No more shortcuts. And no more detours through the Twilight Zone."

"Noted," Tyler replied. "And, for the record, if I die, dump my body in a river or burn it. If those fuckers get ahold of my corpse and turn me into a zombie or something, it's your ass I'll be coming after first."

***

They continued south along the street for nearly a mile before it turned east again. Instead of heading straight back to the highway, the road began to meander back and forth through a wealthy suburb. The houses here were as close to mansions as anything Erik had ever seen – huge, three and four-story stone houses sitting behind wrought-iron fences and gated driveways on two or three-acre lawns. Each had balconies, pillared porches, and tall windows. Most had swimming pools in the backyards and several overlooked an expansive, private golf course.

Erik whistled as he surveyed the neighborhood. "Whew! Got to keep this place in mind if I ever decide to hole up somewhere. Talk about surviving the apocalypse in style!"

"Screw survival," Tyler said. "I'd stay here for the scenery." He nodded towards a mansion a little ways up the road and on the right.

Sitting on a bench swing on the front deck of the biggest, most expensive home in the neighborhood was a barefoot girl who looked to be in her late teens or early twenties. She was slim, with short, dark hair and long, slender legs. She was wearing cut-off jeans and a sleeveless white blouse, showing colorful tattoos on both her upper arms. She was reading a book while swinging lazily back and forth.

Erik had to agree with Tyler. Maybe she wasn't the prettiest girl he had ever seen, but she certainly had to rank in the top ten.

He mentally checked himself. This was the apocalypse after all. How many women were left in the world? To his knowledge, this girl was now the most beautiful woman on the planet.

As they came up even with the closed gate at the end of the driveway, the girl glanced up and saw them. Snapping the book closed, she got to her feet and disappeared into the house.

"I told you to take a bath last night," Erik quipped.

"Eat shit. She went in to tell her mother she's just seen the man she's going to marry."

"Well, of course she did. Unfortunately, it's not you."

Erik looked at the chain and lock holding the gate closed. On a post off to the side was an intercom box.

"Should we ring the buzzer or just walk in and say hi?"

"I don't think the buzzer works." Tyler said. He nodded to the chain and padlock on the front gate. "And I get the feeling they don't like people just walking in." He glanced back to the mansion. "Besides, it looks like we've already been announced."

A man in army fatigues stepped out of the house and onto the front porch. He was short but stocky, built like a wrestler, with brown hair that was cut in a high-and-tight Marine style. He was wearing a pistol on his hip. He stood looking at them and was soon joined by a second soldier, this one taller, thinner, and with dark, curly, almost black hair and a short beard. The second soldier not only had a pistol on his hip but also a military-style rifle slung over his shoulder – most likely an M-16, Erik guessed.

After a brief, whispered discussion, the taller soldier handed his rifle to the shorter one and then started across the lawn and down the driveway towards them. The shorter one stayed on the front deck, keeping the rifle pointed in their general direction but not aiming it at them... yet.

"We could keep walking," Erik suggested. "I mean, how do we know this isn't some Texas chainsaw massacre type of thing? Maybe that girl was only sitting there as bait to lure us in."

"Because this ain't Texas, doofus. And chainsaws don't work anymore. But I will admit, she does make for some pretty tempting bait."

The soldier stopped a few feet from the gate and looked them over, his hand resting on the butt of the pistol at his side.

"Morning. I'm Sergeant Ortiz. You boys here for a reason or are you just out for a stroll?"

"Just passing through," Erik said. "Trying to get back to the highway."

"One-sixty-nine?"

Erik nodded. "Yep."

The soldier, Sergeant Ortiz, considered this and then nodded to the road, "Keep going east for about half a mile. You can't miss it."

These guys didn't want any uninvited guests.

"Well, okay then," Erik said, unsure of what he'd been expecting the soldier to say. He turned back to the road and gave a wave of his hand. "Thanks."

Tyler gave a half-assed salute. "Carry on, sergeant." He turned with Erik.

They had walked only half a dozen steps when the sergeant stopped them.

"Hold on a minute." He stepped closer to the gate. "Where are you boys coming from? Are you local?"

"No, I'm from Iowa," Erik said. "I was up at a camp north of Grand Rapids. Heading back home to Iowa now."

"I'm with him," Tyler said, pointing his thumb to Erik. "But I'm from Aitkin. I'm kind of hanging with him for a ways." He shrugged. "Got nothing better to do."

"You boys look like you've been on the road awhile." He nodded back down the road. "You come by way of the church?"

"We saw it," Erik said. "White, sitting on a hill, couple hundred dead bodies all wrapped up like mummies..."

"Creepy-damn women playing wake-the-dead," Tyler added. "Big fat hillbilly acting like some bored mall cop..."

"How many?" Ortiz asked.

"How many what?" Tyler replied. "Bodies? Women? Men?"

"Men and women."

"One redneck, eight women," Erik replied. "Best guess is over two hundred corpses."

"Did they see you?"

"Not the dead ones," Tyler deadpanned.

"Don't think so," Erik said. "We were hiding behind some bushes."

The sergeant stepped forward and produced a key from his pocket. He unlocked the chain and pulled the gate open.

"You first," he said, nodding to Erik. He kept his hand on the butt of his pistol as he stepped back to allow Erik through. "Got any weapons on you?"

Erik noticed how the other soldier by the house shifted his stance, turning slightly sideways and taking a firmer grip on his rifle. He wasn't looking at only him and Tyler. The soldier was turning his head slightly to the left and the right, scanning the road in front of the mansion, apparently watching for a sudden attack from whoever he and Tyler might be with.

These guys weren't taking any chances.

Erik stepped through the gate and slid his backpack off. "Forty-four-magnum in my pack." He held the pack out to the soldier.

"Just put it on the ground there. Open it up and take a step back."

Erik did as he was told, wondering exactly when it was he'd agreed to be treated as a suspect.

Sergeant Ortiz did a quick search of his backpack. He pulled the pistol out, examined it, and then put it back into the pack. He told Erik to raise his arms and then gave him a quick pat down.

"Seen anyone else on the road?" Ortiz asked.

"An old woman up south of Milaca, but she was sick, probably dead by now. A crazy guy in Aitkin where I met him." He nodded to Tyler. "He's dead too – burned himself up in a fire. And an old man with a cat up in Garrison. He killed himself after his wife died."

The sergeant finished his pat-down, stood, and cocked an eye at him. "You two sure seem to be leaving a trail of death behind you."

"What can I say? It's the end of the world. People are dropping like flies." Erik decided not to tell him about Seth.

"Uh huh," the sergeant said, eyeing him a bit longer before turning to Tyler.

"Okay, now you. Got any weapons on you?"

"Same as him," Tyler said, stepping through the gate. "Pistol in the pack and a swingin' dick in my pants." He took his backpack off and set it beside Erik's.

Sergeant Ortiz did a quick search of his pack, again checking the pistol and then returning it. As he was patting Tyler down, he stopped and pulled the Bowie knife from its sheath on Tyler's belt. He took a step back, holding the knife up.

"Forget about this?"

"Actually, yes," Tyler said, looking genuinely surprised. "Found that in a cabin up around Garrison. I'm not used to wearing it so, yeah, I kind of forgot I had it."

"You guys seem a little paranoid," Erik said. "You worried about that church back there? Are they some kind of cult?"

"We've been watching them," Ortiz said. "Not sure yet how much of a threat they are. They pretty much keep to themselves. But you definitely don't want to approach them. There's more than one man with them and they seem pretty well armed. All we've seen them do so far is fire warning shots if we get too close but that could change." He handed Tyler's knife back to him. "You boys are free to go if you want. Or you can come on up to the house and stay a while. I know Saundra will want to meet you but it makes no difference to me."

"Why check us for weapons and then let us keep them?" Tyler asked, sliding his knife back into its sheath. "Are we really that non-threatening?"

"We just want to know who we're dealing with. Besides, if you'd been with that cult or part of some survivalist group looking to deal us some trouble, you would have lied to me or resisted being searched, and then Corporal McClain up there would have had to shoot you." He glanced to the soldier on the deck and then back to them and grinned. "Just between you and me, I'm glad he didn't have to shoot. He's not that good and he probably would have hit me."

Erik couldn't tell if he was joking or not. Either way, he got the distinct impression it would not be good to mess with these guys.

They picked up their backpacks and Sergeant Ortiz led them up to the house.

The soldier on the front deck, Corporal McClain, relaxed as they approached and introduced himself.

"You boys been living on the road awhile?" he asked, shaking their hands.

"Three weeks at least," Erik said. "I don't know. What's the date?"

"July the tenth."

Erik did a quick calculation in his head. "Closer to four weeks then. Ever since the world went to hell."

"Well, come on in," McClain said. "Bet you haven't had a hot shower or a hot meal in a long while. We've got both."

As the soldiers stepped aside for them to enter the house, Erik felt a curious sense of unease, as though once he crossed the threshold, he might never want to leave again.

***

They were welcomed into the house by Saundra, who had been standing inside the front door the whole time, watching and listening as the soldiers verified the boys posed no threat. She was a tall, slender, middle-aged black woman with graying hair. It was immediately apparent to Erik that, while Sergeant Ortiz and Corporal McClain were in charge of security, it was Saundra who was firmly in charge of this house.

After insisting that they stay for dinner and spend the night, Saundra requested that McClain escort them immediately up the stairs and to the showers.

"These boys have fifty miles of road on them and I won't have it on my floors or at my table. And for heaven's sake, take those packs out to the back porch before something crawls out of them."

Erik was pleasantly surprised to find not only soap and shampoo in the bathroom he was assigned – the house had at least four – but also toothpaste, a toothbrush, floss, deodorant, and a variety of skin creams and moisturizers. He didn't care much for the creams and moisturizers but he planned to put everything else to good use. He hadn't brushed his teeth since the day before the storm and his breath probably smelled like an open sewer.

He spent a little longer in the hot shower than he thought he probably should, but since no one hollered at him to get out, he didn't feel too guilty about it. When he stepped out of the shower, his old clothes had mysteriously disappeared and been replaced by fresh, clean ones.

McClain showed him to their assigned bedroom where Tyler was already peering into the closets, opening the dresser drawers, and checking out the patio door that opened onto a second-floor balcony.

"This place is awesome," Tyler exclaimed, turning back from the balcony. "Remember when I told you I might dump your ass if we come across civilization? Well, buddy, you're in serious danger of being dumped." Then to McClain he asked, "How is it you have hot water here when the rest of the world has only cold, if any at all?"

"You can thank Sergeant Ortiz for that. He was a plumber in his previous life. This community has its own private water tower as well as a small lake – one of the perks of being rich, I suppose – and Ortiz closed off all other lines but the one coming into this house. He also rigged up a propane boiler system in the basement that supplies both heat and hot water."

"What about these clothes?" Erik asked, indicating his new, clean t-shirt, jeans, and sneakers. He'd noticed that Tyler was also wearing clean clothes and new shoes after his shower. "You can't tell me the owners of this house just happened to have two boys exactly our sizes."

McClain laughed. "You stay here a while and you'll learn that when Saundra says 'jump,' you just do it. You don't even ask, 'how high?' There's a second-hand store down the road. She sized you up the moment you walked in the door. Even before you were in the showers, she gave me your sizes and had me run down there and pick out some new clothes for you. Hope you weren't attached to your old ones. They're burning in the dumpster out back as we speak – Saundra's orders."

"So, this is Saundra's house?" Erik asked.

"Technically, it's Doctor Barrett's house but Saundra runs it. Doctor Barrett was a neurosurgeon over in Minneapolis. Saundra's a registered nurse. She was a live-in home-health aid for his wife. From what I gather, Barrett's wife died a couple of years ago and Saundra stayed on to look after him. He's eighty-eight and confined to a wheelchair now. You'll meet him later. He's been going downhill pretty fast these past couple of weeks. I don't think he's got much longer."

"What about that girl?" Tyler asked. "The one we saw on the porch. I haven't seen her around since we got here."

"Ah… Ashley. No, you probably won't see her around until dinner. But don't get your hopes up. She's a little closed off. She doesn't talk about her past much so I guess it wasn't a happy one. All I know is she came up from Minneapolis. She said it's turned into a real hellhole. I guess there were some plane crashes and stuff that started fires and now the whole city is pretty much a smoking ruin. Anyone left there is either in some roving gang or hiding from the gangs."

"Jeeze," Erik said. "How did she get out?"

McClain shook his head. "She never said. But she was with that cult you saw for a few days before she showed up here. We've never gotten her to talk much about that either. When she's not helping Saundra out around the house, she keeps pretty much to herself, either reading books on the porch swing or out on one of the balconies staring off into the distance."

As he resumed their tour of the house, the corporal explained how he and Sergeant Ortiz had been stationed up at Fort Riley, northwest of Elk River. After the storm, they headed for Minneapolis. They came across Saundra in a pharmacy stockpiling medicines and medical supplies and had accepted her invitation to stay with her and Doctor Barrett for a couple of days.

As they were getting ready to move on to Minneapolis, Ashley showed up and informed them the city was in ruins. Trucks, cars, trains, and jets had crashed all over the city the night of the storm. With no emergency crews to respond, the flames spread quickly. The resulting firestorm reduced most of downtown Minneapolis to ash and rubble within days. There were a few survivors here and there, Ashley said, but they had been reduced to their most basic survival instincts – clawing, fighting, and killing each other for a bottle of water or a can of food.

"She must be pretty tough," Tyler said.

"She is," McClain replied. "She's also smart and she's got good instincts. If anyone is going to survive this mess, I'd put my money on Ashley."

"So, what are you doing now?" Erik asked. "Holing up here, waiting for… what?"

"For now, our goal is simply to survive the first year – gather enough supplies to get us through the winter. In the spring... I don't know, maybe head south, maybe stay put and try to build up something here. Unfortunately, there's no standard operating procedure on what to do when civilization goes belly-up. None that I was ever told about, anyway."

In the master bedroom on the first floor, they found Saundra spoon-feeding hot broth to a small, frail looking old man propped up against a pile of pillows in his bed. He was mostly bald, with a few long strands of white hair still clinging to his scalp. His skin was a dark, leathery brown and his eyes were dull, milky white, and sunken. Erik recognized his condition. He didn't look as bad as the old woman who had attacked them but he was definitely suffering from the same post-storm illness.

Saundra permitted Corporal McClain to introduce them to Doctor Barrett and him to them. The doctor made no indication he was even aware of their presence. After the brief introductions, Saundra shooed them from the room and McClain closed the door behind them.

"We saw a woman who looked like that up around Milaca," Erik said after they had left the room. "It's like whatever killed off most everyone else instantly, it's affecting some people more slowly."

"Saw a deer like that too," Tyler added. "Almost barbequed itself in our campfire."

"Doctor Barrett thinks it was some kind of radiation," McClain said, "but not like anything anyone's ever seen before. He studied it the best he could before he started going downhill, even taking samples of his own blood and skin."

"Does that mean we're all going to eventually end up like him?" Tyler asked.

"He didn't think so. His theory is that if you got a full dose of the radiation, you died instantly, becoming one of those mummified corpses. But if all you got was a small dose, like him, then you die more slowly. And if you're not showing any symptoms by now, then you're one of the lucky few who got only a tiny dose or none at all."

"Does he have any theories on where it came from?" Erik asked.

"He's pretty sure it was cosmic, that it came from space. Some random event like a coronal mass ejection or gamma ray burst, but more likely something we didn't even know existed out there. It hit the other side of the earth, most likely sterilizing it of all life in less than a second."

"He saw it too?" Erik asked.

McClain nodded. "He said he was awake and looking at the stars through his telescope the night it happened. He described it as a brilliant flash followed by an extreme disturbance to the earth's magnetosphere. Whatever it was, I guess it was just dumb luck it hit the daytime side of the planet, and that some of us on the night side happened to be in the right place at the right time to survive whatever radiation made it through."

"Just think if you hadn't gotten up that night to take a piss," Tyler said to Erik.

"Believe me," Erik replied, picturing Connor's dead eyes staring at him from across the tent. "That's something I'm going to think about the rest of my life."

***

Erik and Tyler stopped inside the doorway to the dining room and stared with open mouths at the table in front of them. It was set for six, with a white linen tablecloth, linen napkins, and lighted candles down the center of the table. There was a big, steaming bowl of linguini with white clam sauce, bowls of hot vegetables and mixed fruit, small plates of diced cheeses, a platter holding a thick loaf of garlic bread, and bottles of red wine set around the table.

"Holy shit," Tyler breathed. "This is like… *real* food!"

"There will be no gutter-talk at *my* table, young man," Saundra admonished him as she was setting out the last of the silverware. "If you want to use language like that, I'll fix a plate for you and you can eat on the back porch."

Ashley was helping Saundra set the table. She didn't look up at them but Erik saw her suppress an amused smile at Tyler's *faux pas*.

Tyler mumbled an apology.

"It's probably not as fancy as what you're used to eating on the road," Sergeant Ortiz said, "but we do muddle along the best we can."

"I didn't think I would ever see a real table setting again," Erik said. "This looks… incredible."

Saundra deferred all complements to Ashley. "She is certainly a blessing to an over-worked old woman. I don't know what I would do without her."

As they took their seats at the table, Ortiz and McClain stood behind Saundra and Ashley and helped them with their chairs, a formality Erik had seen only in old movies and one he was sure Saundra had drilled them in. There were going to be no elbows allowed on this table and all napkins had better be placed on laps.

Saundra said grace and then excused herself from the table to attend to the doctor, who was apparently going downhill much faster now. Ashley offered to go with her but Saundra insisted she stay at the table and enjoy her meal.

As they ate, Corporal McClain quizzed the boys on their journey to date.

"I've got nothing," Tyler said. "I was sitting on my butt drinking booze, eating beef jerky and chips, and reading comic books for two weeks until Mr. Adventure here showed up." He pointed toward Erik with his thumb.

Erik explained about his time at camp. He intended to leave out exactly what type of camp it was and why he was there, but Tyler brought it up and so he told them the same version of the story he'd told Tyler in the barn.

"He was pushing other kids around and I told him to stop. He got in my face and gave me a shove, so I hit him. Nothing much more than that."

"Broke his jaw with one punch and put him in the hospital," Tyler said. "Don't mess with the kid from Iowa."

Erik told them about the time he'd spent in Grand Rapids and went on to explain how he'd come across Seth, their journey south to Aitkin where they'd found Tyler and Crazy Bob, and then about the barn, the horse, and the accident that had cost Seth his life.

"It was a freak accident, like how some people survived the storm. If he hadn't been standing right there, right at that moment when the wire snapped…" Erik had to stop and look down at his plate. He thought he would be over Seth's death by now. He wasn't.

Sergeant Ortiz, sitting on the other side of Erik, placed his hand on Erik's shoulder. "You did your best. You went out of your way to take him with you and to help him. It wasn't anyone's fault. Like you said, it was nothing more than a freak accident."

Tyler finished up the story of their journey by telling them about their time in Garrison with Nils and his stray cat, the crazy woman who had tried to kill them, the sick deer along the creek bed, and about how they had solved the mystery of the missing mummies right there in Elk River.

"So, what are they doing with all those bodies?" Tyler asked. "It looked like they were trying to resurrect them or something."

"We should defer to our resident cult expert," McClain said. "Ashley spent a few days with them."

"I'm hardly an expert," she said, glancing down and twirling her linguini with her fork.

It was the first time Erik had heard her speak. She looked uncomfortable at suddenly being the center of attention.

When she didn't say anything more, McClain went on to answer Tyler's question.

"They call themselves the Daughters of God. From what we've seen and what Ashley told us earlier, it's an all-woman's group, maybe a dozen of them in all, plus the men they use as labor and bodyguards."

"Daughters of God?" Tyler smirked. "Really? So, they're a bunch of DOGs?"

"I don't think they considered the acronym before naming themselves," Ortiz said. "I guess their leader, Sister Angie, had some kind of vision that the corpses aren't dead, that they're only sleeping until Jesus returns and raises them up again. They call the mummies 'the blessed sleepers.'"

"So, they're… what?" Erik asked. "These women are trying to resurrect the bodies themselves? Awaken the sleepers?"

"Cleansing them of their sins," Ashley said, deciding to speak again. "They pray over the bodies, asking forgiveness for their sins. Sister Angie thinks God is preparing for a new heaven and earth. I guess it says that in the bible somewhere. So, for some reason, he put everyone into this deep sleep until Jesus gets here and sorts everything out."

"That makes like no sense at all," Tyler said.

"What about us?" Erik asked. "Or them? How do they explain everyone who's still alive, or not 'sleeping?'"

"She thinks herself and her followers are here to watch over the sleepers – caretakers, if you will. As far as everyone else that's up and walking around, they think we're demons who've possessed the bodies of the sinful. That's why they'll have nothing to do with us. It's also another reason they pray over the bodies. Angie thinks if they cleanse the bodies of sin, it will keep any more demons from possessing the sleepers and walking the earth."

"I don't feel like a demon," Tyler said. "But if it keeps them away from me…"

"They let you in with them for a while," Ortiz said. "Why didn't they think you were a demon?"

"They *barely* let me in but I don't think they were ever too sure about me. I think it was only because I'm female. It's an all-girl cult, after all. But even then, they kept an eye on me and treated me like a leper. Whenever they brought bodies into the church to wash before wrapping them up, I had to stand in the back next to one of the men. I guess so he could kill me if I suddenly went all exorcist on them."

"So, they really are bodyguards?" Erik asked. "Like hired security?"

"I got the impression the women think the men are angels here to protect them. What's weird is that the women don't talk to the men. They virtually ignore them. And the men don't talk to the women. The men do all the work, like bringing the bodies out of the houses, collecting food and supplies, but there's no real interaction between the two groups."

"That is bizarre," Tyler said. "If those men are angels, why do they dress like rednecks and carry rifles? Hell, I bet that fat one we saw even chews tobacco. Why aren't they all dressed in shiny armor and carrying flaming swords like proper angels?"

"Cults don't have to make sense," McClain said, "at least, not to outsiders. I'll bet Sister Angie or one of the other women did talk to the men at first and that's how the separation of duties got established. But thinking the rest of us are demons… That's what has me a little worried."

"Why?" Erik asked.

"What do angels do best?" Ortiz asked.

After a pause when no one answered, he finished. "They slay demons."

***

After dinner, Erik and Tyler tried to help with the dishes but were promptly chased out of the kitchen by Saundra.

"I may live up north now," she said, "but I was born and raised proper in southern Georgia. You men may think you rule the world and you're welcome to it, but you certainly do *not* belong in my kitchen."

The boys retreated to the sitting room where Sergeant Ortiz was relaxing in a chair with a glass of whiskey and an amused smile on his face.

"Made the mistake of going into the kitchen, didn't you? Stick around and you'll learn soon enough. It may be a man's world but this is most definitely Saundra's house. She calls the shots around here."

They each took a seat in front of the fireplace with Ortiz. He offered them each a small glass of whiskey. "Keep it to a minimum," he advised. "You get all goofy and Saundra will hang me out to dry."

"Where's the corporal?" Erik asked. He took a sip of whiskey and almost gagged from the burn in his throat. He struggled to keep it down.

Ortiz lifted his glass with one finger pointing straight up. "The attic. There's kind of a crow's nest up there, with windows all around. We take shifts, all night, every night."

"How can you see anything?" Tyler asked, glancing to the dark windows.

"We can't. But neither can anyone else. If someone was trying to sneak up on us, he would have to be using a lantern or some other light. In this darkness, you can spot a birthday candle a mile away from up there."

"Who are you watching for?" Erik asked. "That cult?"

"Them, survivalists, anyone who might be thinking we've got something they want." Ortiz took a sip of his whiskey. "It might seem pointless, with so few people around now, but if you get into the habit of letting your guard down, that's when bad things can happen."

They talked for a while longer until Saundra came in and shooed Erik and Tyler off to bed. She cast a stern look at the two empty whiskey glasses on the table and then to the sergeant.

Tyler fell asleep within minutes. Erik, however, found himself wide awake. Taking a lantern, he slipped through the sliding glass doors that opened onto the balcony. It stretched all the way across the front of the house. There was a small, wrought-iron table on the balcony with three matching, padded chairs. He set his lantern on the table, keeping the flame low, and then walked over and leaned forward on the railing, staring out into the darkness.

He thought the night air should be cool and refreshing. It wasn't. It was cool but still as dank and stale as in the daytime.

Since dinner, his thoughts had been on Seth and how different things would be if he'd survived for only a few days longer.

Back in Aitkin, when Tyler had asked him if he was going to take Seth all the way to Iowa with him, he had said he would unless he could find a community or group of survivors where the boy could stay. And here it was, the perfect home for a ten-year-old boy who had lost his entire family and the world as he knew it. Saundra would have doted on him like a mother hen. McClain and Ortiz would have been like uncles to him. And Ashley probably would have treated him like a little brother.

Seth could have been happy here.

He felt like crying but all his life he'd been taught that men don't cry, and he found himself holding it back without even understanding why. He wanted to cry. Seth deserved it. But he couldn't.

He heard the doors leading out to the balcony slide open and then closed again. He assumed it was Tyler, having woken up, coming out to see what he was doing. He quickly composed himself and then realized the sound had come from the other side of the balcony, where a different bedroom opened onto it.

He glanced over as Ashley was stepping up to the railing beside him. She didn't say anything at first, didn't even look at him. She leaned forward on the railing and joined him in staring out into the utter blackness of the night.

Erik had previously seen her tattoos only from a distance. Now, by the dim light of the lantern, he could see them more clearly. On her upper right arm was a raven encircled by barbed wire. On her left was a bluebird perched on a twirling, leafy vine with a single white flower. He found the contrast interesting and guessed they probably symbolized something personal to her. Maybe he would ask her about them some time, but not right now.

They stood there for a couple of minutes, both leaning on the railing and staring out into the darkness before Ashley broke the silence.

"If thou gaze long into an abyss," she said quietly, "the abyss will also gaze into thee."

Erik took a second to run that through his head.

"That sounds familiar."

"It's Friedrich Nietzsche. He was a German philosopher." Ashley cast him a quick glance and Erik noticed for the first time that she had green, almost feral eyes. She nodded back to the darkness. "What do you see in the abyss, Erik?"

He sighed, staring back into the night. "I was thinking that Seth would have liked it here. This would have been a good home for him."

"You don't think he would have wanted to stay with you, to go with you all the way to Iowa?"

Erik thought about it. "I don't know. Maybe. I wouldn't have minded if he did. But I thought it would be better if I found a place for him he could call home. You know, around other people, with a roof over his head. Not living on the road, scavenging for supplies, sleeping in old barns and dry creek beds. He deserved a real home."

She was quiet for a while and then turned to look at him.

"Are you and Tyler going to stay?"

Erik grinned and shook his head. "Tyler might. He's been telling me since I met him that he's going to dump my ass at the first sign of civilization. I think this place is as close to civilization as anything we're going to find."

"But you're not staying."

"I'll probably stay a day or two, if it's okay with you guys. But I have to keep going."

Ashley went back to looking out over the railing and didn't ask any more questions for a while. Erik was about to excuse himself and go back to bed when she spoke again.

"The woods are lovely, dark and deep. But I have promises to keep, and miles to go before I sleep." She paused and then looked at him again. "That's from a poem by Robert Frost."

"I like it."

"What promise do you have to keep?" she asked, her feral green eyes searching his own.

Erik hesitated. Was she really that intuitive, or was he just that easy to read? He could see what McClain had meant when he'd said that Ashley was smart as well as tough. He had the feeling that if he lied to her, she would know it instantly and probably never talk to him again.

"I'm sorry," she said, seeing his hesitation. She glanced back out over the railing. "I'm probably getting too personal."

"No," he said quickly, not wanting her to shut down and close him off. "You're right. I did make a promise. To my sister."

She looked at him again, her eyes sparkling in the light of the lantern.

"She's eight years old," Erik continued. "I've practically raised her since my parents separated a few years ago. She was pretty upset when I had to leave for camp. I promised I would come back to her."

"What's her name?"

"Samantha, but she likes to be called Sam." Erik smiled. "We were reading *Alice's Adventures in Wonderland* before bed every night. I promised her we would finish it when I got home."

"Is she the real reason you had to go to that camp?"

He hesitated again. Damn, she was better than his mother at reading his mind. Did all women have this ability? He shook his head.

"No, it wasn't her fault."

"But it was *because* of her, wasn't it? You broke that other kid's jaw and gave him a concussion. You put him in the hospital with one punch. You don't hit someone that hard just for pushing other kids around, kids you barely even know, unless you're some kind of sociopath. That took real fury."

He looked back out into the night. It was no use. She already knew. She just didn't know the details.

"He pushed her down," he said. "Sam was running in the hall with a friend of hers. You know, like little kids do. They were laughing about something and running, not paying attention to where they were going. They came around the corner and Sam ran right into this guy. Before she could even apologize or say anything, he pushed her down, really hard. I was standing right there and when I saw that... when I saw the look in her eyes..."

He shook his head. "I don't know. I think I could have killed him right then. I remember this feeling exploding inside of me – anger, *rage*. The next thing I knew I was standing over him and he was unconscious on the floor, blood pouring from his mouth. I thought I *had* killed him."

Ashley didn't say anything for a while. Erik was ready for another quotation but it never came.

After a while, she nodded slightly and said, "I think you did the right thing. I know nowadays everyone would say you should have gone to a teacher or the principal or someone so everyone could talk it out and share their feelings and crap. But for your sister, right then, right there, you did exactly the right thing."

She pushed herself off the railing and turned to him and smiled.

"I like you, Erik. I wish I would have known you before the end of the world. It seems like such a waste that I didn't."

She turned and walked back to her room, glancing briefly over her shoulder to say "Goodnight" before slipping through the sliding doors and closing them behind her.

Erik stayed on the balcony a few minutes longer, thinking about how he would like to talk to her some more before he left. He felt there was much more to her than met the eye, but he still knew nothing about her. This whole time they had talked only about him. She was still as much a mystery as when he first saw her on the porch swing that morning.

JULY 11

Dr. Barrett died during the night.

Erik and Tyler pitched in to help McClain and Ortiz dig a grave in the backyard. Saundra sewed a heavy quilt around his body and they buried him next to what had once been a rose garden off to the side of the yard. Of the dozens of rose bushes in the garden, a single rose near the back was still alive and in bloom.

Sergeant Ortiz gave a short eulogy, reading passages from a bible.

Saundra, who was the only one of them who had known both the doctor and his wife, said a few departing words while everyone else stood in respectful silence. Tears ran freely down her cheeks as she spoke. Ashley held her hand throughout and Erik saw that she too was crying. He suspected Ashley's tears were more in sympathy for Saundra than for the loss of the good doctor.

After the funeral, Saundra retreated into the house and Ashley followed. McClain and Ortiz approached Erik and Tyler.

"How do you boys feel about accompanying one of us on a supply run today?" McClain asked.

"It would help us out a lot," Ortiz added. "Usually, only one of us can go while the other stays behind to watch over the place, and one person can't haul a whole lot of supplies in a single trip, so it ends up being an all-day job."

"Not a problem," Tyler said.

"Yeah, sure," Erik agreed. "We might as well help you restock some of the supplies we've been using up."

McClain led them to a garden shed in the back where a large, black, yard wagon was stored.

"We call this the mule. Makes for fewer trips but don't let the name fool you. It's just a big damn wagon. We're the mules."

As they dragged the mule out of the shed, Sergeant Ortiz came out of the house holding two M-16 rifles. He handed one to Erik and the other to Tyler.

"Pistols are fine for close-up defense and they're easy to carry and conceal, but they're shit for long range. If that cult or some survivalist group sees us and wants to take what we have, you'll be damn glad you have one of these."

"Like I have any idea how to use this," Tyler said, frowning at the weapon in his hands.

McClain used his own rifle to show him how to lock and load the weapon as well as how to put it on safety and to switch between semi-automatic and fully automatic fire. He then had Tyler run through the steps a couple of times with his own rifle and fire off a few practice shots to get the feel of the weapon.

"This is just for a worst-case scenario," McClain cautioned them. "I don't expect you to be an instant marksman or anything. Seriously, if something happens and bullets start flying, get your heads down and leave the shooting to me."

"Then why even have us carry these?" Tyler asked

"Because if I get killed, you're on your own. Skilled or not, at least you'll be able to shoot back and maybe, by accident, wing one of 'em." He looked at Erik. "How about you?"

Erik pulled the charging handle back to load the weapon, checked to make sure it was on semi-automatic, and then aimed and fired at the row of tin-can targets set up against the fence. He fired twice, hitting two cans.

McClain was impressed. "You've got experience with one of these?"

"My dad was a cop. We used to go out to the shooting range all the time. We usually shot pistols but every now and then he'd break out his .30-.06 or the AR-15, which is basically the same rifle as this except for the full-automatic setting."

Ortiz pointed to a streetlight along the side of the road. "That light is about two hundred yards away. Think you can hit it?"

Erik got down on one knee and sighted in on the light. He pulled the trigger, firing a single shot. The light exploded and glass rained down on the street below. He stood up and put the weapon back on safety.

"Fucking A!" Tyler exclaimed.

"I think he might be better than you," Ortiz said to McClain.

"Better than you too," McClain replied. "Okay. Good deal then. Hopefully, seeing that we're armed with automatic weapons will cause anyone to think twice about messing with us. But if we do run into trouble, follow my lead. And remember, aim and fire with short, controlled bursts. No more than three shots at a time. Don't go full auto unless you're strafing a hedgerow or something. Otherwise, you're just wasting ammo."

Erik slung the rifle over his shoulder and caught a glimpse of movement up by the house. He looked and saw Ashley disappearing back through the door. He guessed she'd heard the shooting and came out to see what was going on. It occurred to him that, with as little as anyone knew about her, maybe she could shoot better than all of them. Hell, it wouldn't surprise him to find out she had been a trained assassin in her life before the storm.

They set out on the road. Corporal McClain pulled the mule while Erik and Tyler walked along either side of him. Sergeant Ortiz stayed behind to complete the morning walk-around of the mansion grounds, a routine they completed four times a day.

After walking for over an hour up one street and then down another, they came to an industrial area of town along the highway that held a dozen or so warehouses and storage sheds. Multiple tractor-trailer rigs and several delivery vans were parked in the lots and spaces between the buildings.

They stopped at the top of a rise in the road, looking down on the warehouses.

"This is a distribution center," McClain said. "Companies used it to store merchandise prior to orders being shipped out." He pointed to a warehouse on the end with a large number 4 painted on the side. "That's the one we want."

Erik expected them to immediately head down to the warehouse but McClain stood where he was, looking down on the buildings. "What are we doing?" he asked.

"Just watching. Making sure nothing has changed since we were here last. Looking for open doors or signs that someone else might be here. If someone else finds this place, they may try to stake a claim to it and move in."

After a few minutes of studying the warehouse and the lot, McClain said, "Okay, let's go," and began pulling the mule forward again.

Warehouse number 4 was filled with row upon row of tall, steel storage racks loaded down with cases of boxed and canned food as well as cases of household items like toothpaste, soap, paper towels, and nearly everything else one would find in the aisles of a grocery store.

"This looks like the mother lode," Tyler said. "And here we've been scavenging people's leftovers from their cupboards and pantries all this time."

"This is only one supply warehouse we know of," McClain said. "There are a couple more but we haven't had to use them yet." He pulled a thick square of paper out of his pocket and unfolded it. "This is basically a map of where everything is stored in here. I found it in the warehouse office and it seems to be mostly accurate." He pulled another, smaller sheet of paper from his other pocket. It was a hand-written list on notebook paper.

"And this is Saundra's shopping list. Match up the list to the map and we should be out of here in an hour."

Erik took the list and Tyler took the map. With Corporal McClain pulling the mule, they went up and down the aisles of the warehouse pulling boxes down and loading them into the wagon. In less than an hour, they had completed the list and the mule was loaded down enough to where Erik and Tyler had to help push while McClain pulled.

Outside the warehouse, as McClain pulled the door down and locked it again, Erik leaned back on the overloaded mule and rubbed his aching arms. He knew he was in excellent shape from walking for so many miles over the past four weeks or so, but he hadn't done much work with his arms or back until now.

Tyler placed his hands on his hips and leaned back, stretching his spine. He groaned. "Damn. We keep this up and I'm going to either look like a body builder or find my ass in a wheelchair."

"Heads up," McClain said, coming up behind them. He nodded toward a row of houses on a rise to the west. "Looks like we've got a couple of shadows."

Erik had to look carefully back and forth a couple of times before he saw what McClain was talking about. Two men were standing in front of one of the houses up on the hill. The larger one looked as though he was holding a pair of binoculars to his eyes.

McClain pulled his own small pair of binoculars from the cargo pocket of his pants. He peered back at the men for several seconds before handing them to Erik.

"Either of those men look familiar?"

Erik trained the binoculars on the hill. The larger one was the fat man from the church. He didn't recognize the other. The fat man was peering back at them while the other was idly glancing around. Both were armed with rifles and pistols. He handed the binoculars to Tyler so he could also look.

"That big hillbilly," Erik said. "He was at the church."

"Right," McClain said. "The other one is with the cult too. I recognize both of them."

"Shit," Tyler said as he looked through the binoculars. "If they didn't know about this warehouse before, they sure as hell know about it now." He handed the binoculars back to McClain. "What do we do about that?"

"Nothing we can do. They're too far away to shoot us or for us to shoot them. Let's get this stuff back to the house. I don't think they'll try anything but we don't want to let our guard down, either."

"Do you think they'll make a move on the warehouse?" Tyler asked. "Try to claim it for their own?"

"It's possible. But, like I said, we've got a couple of others we haven't even touched yet. If they want to lay claim to this one, we might let them. It'll keep them away from the other two."

"And if they find the others and lay claim to those too?" Erik asked.

"Then we will definitely have a problem," McClain said grimly.

***

"Are you shitting me?" Tyler exclaimed. "I thought you said we were out of supplies."

The rec room in the basement of the mansion was stacked nearly to the ceiling with cases of the same supplies they had just hauled from the warehouse. Along the back wall were dozens of rifles, pistols, and cases of ammunition and gunpowder – the missing inventory from the sporting goods and gun stores, including the BB guns.

"Never said we were out of supplies," McClain replied as he and Ortiz stacked the boxes. "We replace whatever we use, usually about once a week."

"Keep your supplies topped off and you avoid desperate situations," Ortiz added.

"Can't argue with that," Erik said. "But, dang! You could hole up in here for months and never go hungry."

"Seriously," Tyler said, waving his hand at the wall of rifles. "Do you really need all these weapons? There are only two of you. Are you expecting an invasion or reinforcements?"

"Hope for the best, plan for the worst," Ortiz said.

"Besides," McClain added, "if we have all the weapons, that means the enemy doesn't."

"Who's the enemy?" Erik asked. "The cult?"

"Anyone who thinks they can take what we have."

"And the BB guns?" Tyler asked. "Seriously?"

"If it comes down to shooting small game for survival," Ortiz said, "birds, squirrels, rabbits, rats… A decent air gun is perfect. It's quiet and it holds a lot of ammo."

Tyler grimaced. "Rats?"

"It still doesn't make sense," Erik said. "There are only the two of you, maybe three if Ashley knows how to shoot. But I can't see Saundra holding a gun. If you get overrun by a larger group, all these guns and a hundred more won't help you if you don't have enough people to use them."

"No, they won't," McClain agreed. "But we do have a couple of other tricks up our sleeves if it comes to that."

Neither McClain nor Ortiz would explain what "tricks" they had planned.

"It's not that we think you're spies or anything," Ortiz said, "but we have only known you since yesterday. Hell, even Saundra doesn't know everything we're up to and it's her house."

After they'd finished unloading and stacking the supplies, Erik and Tyler went upstairs for lunch while Ortiz and McClain did a walk-through of the immediate neighborhood, something they said they did once every day for general security reasons.

Saundra served them a lunch of vegetable beef soup with crackers, slices of cheese, smoked sausage, and fruit juice before disappearing back into the kitchen. Ashley made only a brief appearance as she crossed through the dining room on her way to some other part of the mansion. She gave them a quick glance and a slight nod as she passed by the table but said nothing.

Tyler watched her disappear around the corner and then said to Erik, "Man, I can see what McClain meant when he said she was closed off. I tried talking to her this morning and it was like asking a rock about its political views."

Erik stuffed a hunk of smoked sausage into his mouth so he wouldn't have to reply and nodded.

"Have you been able to talk to her?"

He continued chewing and shrugged, stalling. He didn't want to mention his conversation with Ashley on the balcony last night. Even though she hadn't told him anything about herself, he felt like even mentioning it would somehow violate her trust. He was saved when Ortiz and McClain came into the room.

Ortiz said something in a low voice to McClain, who veered off and disappeared into the hallway. Ortiz then turned to Erik and Tyler. He had a thoughtful, somewhat concerned, look on his face.

"What's up?" Tyler asked.

"When you're finished, come out on the front porch." Without saying anything more, Ortiz turned and left the room.

Erik and Tyler quickly finished eating and joined him on the porch in front of the house. Ortiz was leaning back against one of the pillars that bracketed the steps, gazing out across the yard to the front gate.

"We've got some unusual activity up at the church."

"You mean something outside of their usual nutty hijinks of stealing corpses and repainting doors?" Tyler asked.

"Normally," Ortiz said, "there are only eight or ten up there at any one time. I think the most we've ever counted all together were twelve but we always knew there could be more." He paused, thinking, and then continued. "They're all up at the church right now, holding some kind of meeting. And there are more of them than we thought. McClain said he counted nine women and six men. There could be more. All the men are heavily armed. He couldn't get closer because they have a couple of guards with rifles positioned outside, something we've never seen them do when the women are inside the church."

"You think they might be planning something," Erik asked, "seeing as they were scouting us out at the warehouse this morning?"

"They've been watching us all along, for at least a week now. We've seen them behind the windows of some of the neighboring houses. We watch them, they watch us. But this morning, they were a little more open about it, didn't even care that we saw them. Between that and this big meeting all of the sudden…"

"Sounds like they're staging up for an assault," Tyler said.

"Right. They know what we've got and they think we're all demons. That's not good." Ortiz pushed himself off the post. "Don't say anything to the girls. It could be nothing. Hell, maybe they're having a big come-to-Jesus meeting. But just in case, keep your weapons loaded and within easy reach until further notice."

After Ortiz had gone back into the house, Tyler looked at Erik.

"Thinking you should have hit the road this morning?"

"I'm back to thinking maybe we should have bypassed this whole town altogether."

After dinner that night, McClain quietly suggested to Erik and Tyler that they go upstairs and become familiar with the layout of the rooms, particularly ones that opened onto the balconies, and all the connecting doors and hallways. McClain himself would stay downstairs in the sitting room, ostensibly relaxing in front of the fire while Ortiz manned the crow's nest.

"You think they'll try something tonight?" Erik asked. "It'll be pitch-black outside in another hour or so."

"Odds are against it," McClain said. He had a glass of what looked like whiskey in his hand but Erik noted it had bubbles in it – some kind of cola. "But when you're dealing with a religious cult and a bunch of bodyguards who look like they used to be in a biker gang, it's probably best to be ready for anything, no matter how unlikely you think it is."

"What would make them suddenly decide to attack now?" Tyler asked. "They've known about this house for weeks, haven't they?"

"Unfortunately, it was probably your arrival," McClain said. "Maybe they think we're building our own numbers up to stage our own attack on them. We are supposed to be demons after all, right?"

Erik and Tyler did as McClain suggested. They took their rifles up to their bedroom and split up, each heading in an opposite direction. To all appearances, Erik hoped, they were simply wandering from room to room, getting acquainted with their new home.

He stepped out onto the balcony and walked from one end to the other, noting how many rooms opened onto it. He stopped at each door to glance in and see if the room had connecting doors. It was almost dark now and he hadn't brought a lantern with him. As he was turning to go back, he was startled to come face-to-face with Ashley standing right behind him.

"Lose something?" Ashley asked, arching her eyebrows.

"No, I was, uh, just checking things out. You know… new place and all. There are a lot of rooms in this house."

"Uh huh. And your buddy, Tyler? Is he just checking things out too?"

"I… suppose so?"

"You can't lie for shit," Ashley said. "You don't think I know something's up? All this whispering… the sergeant going on watch early… the corporal down there pretending to drink whiskey in front of the fire when anyone can see it's soda." Her eyes narrowed as she scrutinized him. "Ever since you guys got back from your little supply run, you've all been acting keyed-up and squirrely."

"It's nothing. It's just that…"

"If you lie to me again, I swear to God I'm going to throw you off this balcony."

He hesitated. He could see in her eyes there was no point in lying to her. And she came across to Erik as someone who didn't make idle threats.

He sighed.

"It's that Daughters of God group. A couple of their so-called angels were watching us today when we went to get the supplies. And now, McClain says there's a big group of them up at the church. He and Ortiz think it's unusual enough that we should be on our guard."

"What does he think they're doing?"

Erik shrugged, hoping he looked calm and unconcerned. "Who knows? Maybe they decided to have a big prayer meeting tonight."

She studied his eyes. "And that's why I saw you and Tyler taking rifles up to your room, because *maybe* they're simply gathering up for a meeting? Bullshit. McClain and Ortiz think those wackos might be heading this way, don't they?"

Erik decided to get it over with. She was going to drag the truth out of him eventually anyway.

"Yeah, but probably not tonight. It's a cult that thinks we're a bunch of demons, okay? They saw two more people arrive and they know there are a bunch of guns and supplies stored in this house. Also, they outnumber us at least three to one. McClain didn't say it but I get the impression he and Ortiz think, if not tonight, it's still only a matter of days before they do try something."

"Like attack us," Ashley stated.

"Yeah."

"And he didn't want ya'll to worry us po' hapless little womenfolk, is that it?" she said in a ditzy southern accent.

Erik felt his face flush. "Well, he didn't say it exactly like that. He just didn't want anyone to worry about something that might not happen."

"And if they do come here, if they attack us tonight, did he happen to mention what his plan is?"

"No, he just said to get familiar with the house and be on our guard."

"Well, if he doesn't have a plan, he'd better get one quick." She nodded toward the road.

Erik turned and saw a procession of lights coming up the road a few hundred yards away, approaching from the direction of the church. He suddenly had a sick feeling in the pit of his stomach.

"Ah, shit."

***

"Time to go," Erik said. Without thinking about it, he put his hand on Ashley's back and all but pushed her into the house.

As they came in from the balcony, Tyler rushed into the room from the hallway.

"You see 'em?" Tyler asked, grabbing his rifle.

"Yeah, they're almost here." He turned to Ashley. "Go downstairs and make sure McClain knows they're coming. Ortiz will already have seen them from the crow's nest."

Without a word, Ashley turned and disappeared out the doorway.

"God damn," Tyler said nervously, checking his rifle. "I hope they're here just to hand out some pamphlets or something, try to talk us out of our sinful ways."

"Don't get too excited yet," Erik said. He pulled the magazine from his rifle, checked it, and then slapped it back in. He pulled the charging handle back and let it slide forward again, locking and loading the weapon. "I didn't see the men, so maybe the women really are coming here to talk. Let's just see what happens but be ready for anything."

Erik took up position against the wall next to the open balcony door and peered out. It was almost full dark now. He could see nine lanterns clustered around the gates at the end of the driveway. By the light of the lanterns, he could make out the robed figures of the women. One was wearing white. The rest were in red.

Tyler took up a position at the window and looked out

"Are they trying the buzzer, or are they waiting for someone to let them in?"

"I don't know," Erik replied. "Maybe if we ignore them, they'll go away and leave a pamphlet stuck in the gate, like the Jehovah's Witnesses."

From the end of the driveway, he heard a dull clunk and then the rattle of the chain as it fell to the ground.

"They cut the lock," Tyler said in a hushed tone.

The gates screeched as they were pushed open and the lights began filing up the driveway toward the house.

"You were saying something about pamphlets?" Tyler asked.

"Let's wait and see what McClain and Ortiz do. It's their call."

"Fuck. I've got to take a piss."

"Me too."

The women approached the house and began to spread out, forming an arc across the front lawn. Sister Angie, their leader in white, took the center of the arc, directly across from the front door. Erik noticed a curious red twinkling coming from multiple locations in the yard and from beneath the trees that bordered the property. They looked like little red stars. The women were standing almost right on top of several but didn't appear to notice them.

"What the hell are those little lights?" he whispered to Tyler.

"They look like reflections off something. Maybe it's an old sprinkler system."

Erik studied them. He didn't think lawn sprinklers would reflect with red light, but he couldn't think of what they might be. Whatever they were, they weren't random. There was about six to eight feet of space between any two of the reflections.

For several minutes, the women stood in front of the house, holding their lanterns in dead silence, not moving, not speaking. The suspense of waiting for what they would do next was unnerving.

"What the fuck are they doing?" Tyler whispered, echoing Erik's own thoughts.

From downstairs, they heard the front door open. Corporal McClain appeared in the yard, walking toward Sister Angie. He held a lantern in his left hand. His right hand was resting on the butt of the service pistol at his hip. He stopped roughly ten feet in front of the leader of the women and said something too low for Erik to hear.

Sister Angie could have been a statue for as much acknowledgment she gave McClain. She was looking past him, staring at the house. There was no emotion in her gaze.

Corporal McClain spoke again. This time Erik heard him say something like, "What do you want?"

The first gunshot came from the left, from back in the trees that bordered the property.

McClain dropped his lantern and spun to the right, almost falling, but then catching himself and running back to the house, drawing his pistol at the same time. He ran with a limp. He had been hit by the shot but not bad enough to drop him.

More shots rang out from different places in the trees, from the left and the right. Erik could hear windows breaking downstairs. The window in front of Tyler exploded.

"Fuck!" Tyler shouted, turning and ducking away from the flying glass.

"Are you hit?"

Tyler was bent over, brushing the glass off his shoulders and head.

"No, but I'm pretty fucking pissed." He stepped to the side of the window and peered around the corner.

"They're in the trees," Erik said. He looked down the sights of his rifle but couldn't find a target. It was too dark out there.

He heard the front door bang closed. McClain must have made it inside. More shots came from the trees, mostly concentrated on the downstairs windows. The women continued to stand in their kind of semi-circle across the front lawn, seemingly oblivious to the bullets that were whizzing past them.

"I can't see shit," Tyler said, aiming his rifle left and then right, looking for a target of his own.

Erik was seeing flashes from within the tree line with every shot. He pointed this out to Tyler.

"Shoot at the muzzle flares."

He tried to sight in on one of the flashes. Before he could pull the trigger, a gunshot sounded from the crow's nest above. It was followed by an almost simultaneous explosion from within the trees.

"Holy shit!" Tyler exclaimed. "What was that?"

There was another shot from Ortiz and another explosion in the trees. Erik wasn't sure, but it seemed to him that both explosions had come from the same places he had seen two of those twinkling red lights.

The men in the trees began firing up at the crow's nest.

Erik took aim and fired at one of the red lights in front of where he saw a muzzle flare. Whatever it was, it exploded in a fireball that lit up the trees. In the flash, he saw one of the cult's bodyguards kneeling beside a tree a few feet away. He shifted his aim and fired three rapid shots. The muzzle flares from that position ceased. Either he had hit him or the man had retreated to another position.

"Shoot at those red lights," Erik shouted to Tyler. "They're grenades or bombs or something."

Tyler took several shots before being rewarded with an explosion of his own. He and Erik began sweeping back and forth through the trees, shooting at the twinkling red lights while Sergeant Ortiz continued raining bullets down from above. By the light of the explosions, they were able to sight in and shoot several of the men in the trees.

Sister Angie stepped forward and began swinging her lantern forward and back. On her cue, the other women also stepped forward and began swinging their own lanterns.

"Shit," Tyler said. "They're going to throw those damn things at the house. They're going to try and burn us out."

Erik aimed at one of the red lights behind Sister Angie and fired. The explosion blew her forward off her feet. She landed in a heap several feet closer to the house, her white robe ablaze.

Two of the other women dropped their lanterns and rushed forward to help her. More shots came from the trees, aimed mostly at the balcony door Erik was shooting from. He ducked to the side. Return fire came from downstairs. The two women rushing to the aid of their leader fell to the ground.

Another shot from Sergeant Ortiz above and another explosion lit up the trees. The remaining women all began hurling their lanterns at the house but the makeshift firebombs all fell short. They were standing too far away. More shots came from Corporal McClain below and another woman fell.

Tyler was shooting rapid-fire into the yard now, sweeping back and forth. He hit one of the red lights and the blast took out another of the women.

The door frame next to Erik's head exploded and he felt hot splinters pepper his forehead. He guessed at where the shot had come from and aimed at a light in the tree line. A muzzle flash appeared behind it and he felt the bullet whiz past his ear. He pulled the trigger and the bomb exploded. In the flash, he saw the fat hillbilly with the cap and suspenders fly back and slam against a tree before thudding to the ground, either unconscious or dead.

Erik and Tyler continued firing at the red lights and muzzle flares while shots continued to ring out from both above and below them. Several more of the bombs exploded in the yard and in the trees. After what felt like twenty or thirty minutes, Erik heard Corporal McClain hollering for a cease-fire.

Erik stepped back and leaned against the wall, wiping his forehead. His hand came away bloody but it didn't look too bad. The silence of the night had returned. There were no more gunshots or explosions. He cautiously peered out past the balcony and down to the yard below.

Most of the lanterns had smashed in the grass. There were small fires spreading everywhere. All nine women lay dead on the lawn. Some were burning. Some were missing body parts from the explosions. Sister Angie was now fully engulfed in flames.

"Burn in hell, bitch," Tyler shouted down at her through the broken window. "Demons rule tonight."

There were fires in and around the surrounding trees. The flickering light illuminated several of the bodyguards lying dead on the ground as well as dozens of shallow craters caused by the explosions.

Erik went over and sat on the edge of the bed. His heart was racing and he suddenly felt weak and jittery.

"I think I'm on adrenaline overload," he said.

Tyler sat next to him. "You and me both." He took a deep breath and blew it out. "I think I have decided not to pursue a career in the military. This shit is way too intense."

Erik checked his rifle and saw he had gone through two and a half clips of ammunition, over thirty bullets. He couldn't remember firing half that many shots, much less changing the clip twice.

Sergeant Ortiz appeared at the bedroom doorway. He glanced at Erik's bloody forehead and the bloody scratches on Tyler's face, neck and arms.

"You boys okay?"

"Got so much adrenaline pumping through me right now I'm probably addicted, but I think I'll survive," Tyler said.

"What the hell were those bombs all over the yard?" Erik asked. "We figured out the reflector trick."

Ortiz grinned. "I saw that. Pretty smart thinking, you two. Yeah, those were one-pound cans of smokeless powder. We buried them shallow all over the yard and put bicycle reflectors over them, angled toward the house so only we could see them. Our plan was that if we were attacked at night, we would throw some oil on the yard and light it up so we could see the reflectors. Conveniently for us, they brought their own light."

"So, that's the secret defense you wouldn't tell us about?" Tyler asked. "Got any more booby-traps hidden around here?"

"No, that was pretty much it. We didn't want to go overboard. But after tonight, I've got a couple more ideas we might try." He turned to leave. "You two come on downstairs and we'll get those cuts tended to. Bring your weapons. This shit may not be over yet."

They followed Ortiz and joined Corporal McClain and the women in the foyer. McClain was bleeding from his right hip and left arm. Saundra was doing her best to make him hold still while she cleaned and inspected his wounds. She turned as Ortiz, Erik, and Tyler entered the room and breathed a visible sigh of relief.

"Thank God you're all okay," she said before turning back to her work.

Ashley grabbed a washcloth from a bucket of water and ran to Erik.

"Jesus! You didn't get shot in the head, did you?"

Erik wiped at his forehead again. "I think it's just splinters. A bullet hit the doorframe next to my head."

Ashley dabbed the cloth against his forehead and then inspected his wounds.

"You've got some nasty scratches but I don't see anything serious. Jesus, you're lucky. Keep this pressed on your head."

She returned to the bucket for another wet rag and administered the same treatment to Tyler's cuts.

"We need to get those fires put out," Ortiz said. "Tyler, grab a bucket of water. Erik, you stay by the window and cover us. I think we got them all but there could be one or two still able to pull a trigger."

While Tyler and Ortiz went outside with buckets of water, Erik knelt by the broken window with the barrel of his rifle resting on the sill. Behind him Saundra was still fussing over McClain.

"This is going to need stitches," Saundra was saying, examining his arm. "Ashley, dear, could you fetch my first-aid kit? It's in my bedroom dresser, top left drawer. And grab some rubbing alcohol from the bathroom." She jumped at the sound of a gunshot from outside.

"It's alright," Erik said. "That was Ortiz." He glanced at McClain, who said nothing but raised his eyebrows a notch.

Saundra didn't ask and he didn't tell her what Sergeant Ortiz was doing outside. Besides putting the fires out, he was also dispatching the survivors of the cult with cold efficiency.

***

Erik dry-heaved into the toilet bowl for the third time that night. Everything in his stomach had already come up about five minutes ago. Visions of the dead and burning women, their body parts strewn all over the lawn, kept resurfacing in glorious Technicolor detail in his head. Each time brought a new round of dry heaves and stomach cramps.

"Fuck," he muttered when his stomach unclenched a little.

As Tyler had put out the fires, Sergeant Ortiz crisscrossed the lawn, dispatching any survivors with a single pistol shot to the head and counting the bodies. When they returned to the house, Ortiz announced that every one of the cult members and their bodyguards were accounted for. "We should be safe tonight," he said. "But just in case, I'll stand watch. I can sleep in the morning."

Saundra stitched Corporal McClain's wounds and forbade him from getting out of bed until she decided he was well enough to move. She then examined Erik's and Tyler's wounds and applied disinfectant and a couple of small bandages over the deeper cuts.

Somewhere between the executions and the first aid, Ashley had disappeared. Erik had not seen her since.

Tyler seemed able to push the horrific scenes of the night completely out of his head. He flopped onto his bed fully dressed and was sound asleep within a couple of minutes.

Erik tried to sleep, but then the visions had come and now he was in the bathroom, kneeling over the toilet and retching like a drunken college student.

After a while his stomach settled down enough to where he was able to stand and lurch over to the sink. He splashed water on his face and gave his teeth a quick brushing. He stared in the mirror. By the flickering light of the lantern, he thought his reflection looked deranged, almost homicidal. He muttered "fuck" again and splashed some more water on his face.

He picked up his lantern and started back to the bedroom. Ashley was standing just outside the bathroom door.

"Jesus," he exclaimed, startled. "Would you quit doing that?"

"Are you alright? I could hear you all the way down the hall. It sounded like you were being sick in there."

"I'm okay. It's just that – I don't know – tonight, with the attack and everything... I guess it was a little too much all at once. Probably overdosed on adrenaline."

"You still look really pale. Come with me."

Ashley took his hand and led him down the hall to the doors leading out onto the balcony. She sat him in one of the padded, wrought-iron chairs and then stood behind him, massaging his neck and shoulders.

"It's not exactly fresh air," she said, "but at least it's cool."

Erik took a couple of deep breaths, letting them out slowly.

"Feeling better?" she asked after a couple of minutes.

He took another breath and let it out. He hadn't realized how much tension and stress he was still carrying until he felt every muscle in his body relaxing. It felt like he'd been wrapped in a strait jacket all night and now the buckles and ties were being loosened.

"Yeah," he said. "That feels good." He loved the feel of her strong fingers kneading his muscles.

She massaged his shoulders for a while longer and then moved to sit in the chair opposite him. She leaned back and looked up at the blackness above, as though forgetting that no stars had been visible since the storm.

"Man, I was so scared," she said. "I thought for sure we were all going to die. I can't imagine what it was like for you guys up here."

"I was scared shitless," Erik admitted. "I'm pretty sure Tyler was too. It all happened so fast and it was so confusing, I don't even remember most of it. What I do remember, it's like something I saw in a movie. You know? Like it happened to someone else."

"That's called disassociation. It's a way of dealing with traumatic events, seeing them as though they're happening to somebody else. Make a habit of it and you'll probably develop a split personality or some other psychosis."

"Gee, that sounds great. It's just what I need on top of everything else."

Ashley continued staring up into the blackness. After a while she said, "You could have left, you know. You could have left yesterday or this morning, or even this afternoon when things were starting to look sketchy." She paused and shifted her gaze to him. "Why did you stay?"

Erik shrugged, not sure what to say. He didn't know why he had stayed. He had not given it any thought at all. It was just something he did.

"You could have been killed," she said. "You can't keep your promise to your sister if you're dead."

"We all could have been killed."

"And now that everyone's safe? Are you going to leave, get back on the road and ride off into the sunset?"

Erik was surprised he still had enough humor left in himself to chuckle.

"Nothing like that. If you haven't noticed, sunsets are a thing of the past and I can't ride anywhere because of my leg. But, yeah, I'll probably head out in a day or so. Not tomorrow but maybe the next day. The weather's turning colder and I'm not even halfway home yet."

"Keep moving forward and all that?"

He nodded.

She stared at him, a curious look in her eyes.

"Who are you, Erik?"

"What do you mean?"

"Are you the hero?"

He hesitated, not sure how to reply. This conversation was taking a strange turn. And she was staring at him with those beautiful green eyes of hers.

"Every story has a hero," she explained. "We're at the end of the world, the biggest story of the last twelve thousand years. It's going to need a hero. So far, it's looking like you."

He gave a short, self-conscious laugh and shook his head.

"I'm not any kind of hero. If I was a hero, I'd be... I don't know. Anything but this." He indicated himself with his hands.

"I'll bet you're a hero to your sister, the way you defend her, read stories to her, keep your promises."

"That's different."

"Is it? And you were Seth's hero. You could have left him there, traumatized and all alone in that town. But you stayed by his side and became his friend. You protected him. You cared for him and tried to find him a new home."

"But I couldn't save him," he said quietly, glancing down.

"But at least you tried. That's more than a lot of people would have done, especially now. And what about Tyler? He said he would probably be dead from alcoholism by now if you hadn't shown up. I see the way he defers to your decisions, follows your lead. I don't think he normally follows anyone."

Erik stared at the floor of the balcony but didn't say anything. He wanted to get off this topic.

"Sorry," Ashley said at last. "I've probably seen too many rom-coms and read too many romantic novels. But you've got to admit, as much as you deny being a hero, everything you do says otherwise."

"I think I'll pass on saving the world," he said, glancing back up. "I wouldn't even know where to begin."

"Maybe you've already begun and you just don't know it."

He decided it was time to change the subject to something other than himself.

"Can I ask you a question?"

She regarded him quietly without replying.

"Your tattoos... I've been wondering what they mean."

She smiled and leaned back in her chair, laying her head back again and gazing up. "You know? You're the first person ever to ask me that. Everyone else either ignores them or says they like them, but no one has ever asked me what they mean." She paused and then asked, "What makes you think they mean anything?"

Erik shrugged. "I don't know. But you don't seem like the kind of person to get a tattoo on a drunken whim or anything."

"Maybe I just like birds."

"A raven wrapped in barbed wire on one arm and a bluebird with a white flower on the other? Looks to me like you're making a statement, telling the world something, like one side of you is trapped while the other is free. Or you feel trapped and you want to be free."

"Pretty intuitive there, hero," she said softly, still gazing up at the starless sky.

She was quiet for a long time after that. Erik thought she wasn't going to say anything more until she gave a deep sigh and continued.

"My sister and I had kind of a rough life growing up – abusive father before he abandoned us, a mother who would rather drink vodka and pass out in front of the TV every night rather than cook dinner or talk to us about our day. When I was younger, I used to escape by reading those sappy romance novels where no matter how bad it got for the heroine, she always had a happy ending after finding her true love. I gave them up after a couple of years but I guess that's where I got the idea every story needs a hero."

She glanced down at the raven on her right arm.

"I got this one when I was still living at home, after my sister left for Minneapolis. I was drinking, smoking dope, hanging out with the wrong sort of crowd. I told people I got it because it looked tough and I hoped it would piss my mom off. But what it really represented was what I thought of myself, like I was this ugly thing that no one wanted, trapped in a miserable life I never asked for.

"I left home when I was seventeen and moved up to the city to live with my sister. She helped me get a job and start cleaning my life up. That's when I got this one." She touched her fingers to the bluebird on her other arm, smiling. "When I got it, I decided if the raven represented my past, I wanted this bluebird to represent my future, the way I wanted my life to be. The flower is my sister but I never got the chance to tell her that." She leaned back and looked up again.

"I almost made it. I really thought I was turning my life around. I was feeling good about it. And then I wake up one morning only to find my sister dead, the city on fire, and the whole world gone to hell."

She gave a humorless laugh and glanced back to Erik.

"What kind of tattoo do you think I should get for that?"

"I think they can still work," he said. "Maybe the raven can be the world we're in now and the bluebird can be hope for the future."

She smiled. "I think you have a lot more hope for the future than I do." She stood up. "But it's your world now and the rest of us are just trying to survive in it. Are you feeling better?"

He wasn't sure how to reply to her comment about this being his world so he didn't even try.

"At least I don't feel like I'm going to puke anymore."

"Good, because I think we're going to have a pretty busy day tomorrow."

JULY 12

"Wow!" Tyler said, standing on the front porch with Erik and looking out over the front lawn. "This looks like the ending credits of some zombie-apocalypse horror movie."

The bloody and burned bodies of robed women lay all over the lawn. Here and there between them was an arm, a foot, an entire leg, or some other undiscernible body part. There were broken lanterns, areas where the dry grass was scorched black, and at least two dozen small craters from the buried cans of gunpowder. The cult's bodyguards, their weapons, and more body parts lay scattered throughout the tree line. Some of the larger trees were scarred and scorched by the bombs while smaller trees and bushes were uprooted, splintered, or burned to their stumps.

The house itself had taken some damage but nothing serious. The porch railing they were leaning against was chipped and splintered, as were the doors and the sills and frames of the shattered windows. The side of the house was pock-marked with bullet holes. At least one of the lanterns hurled by the women – probably the one thrown by Sister Angie herself, since she had gotten the closest – had hit the house but it had done little damage other than to scorch some of the bricks.

Erik had no words. He stood at the railing with Tyler, looking out over the carnage and feeling a kind of hopeless sadness. Even in the wake of the greatest disaster modern man had ever known, the few survivors were still killing each other in the name of religion or for simple possessions. He wondered how they had ever gotten this far, and was this finally the end?

Was nature, at last, sick of their shit and bringing the final curtain down on mankind?

Sergeant Ortiz stepped out of the front door and joined them on the porch. After a quick glance over the yard he said, "We can use the mule. We'll load up the bodies and haul them back to their church."

Corporal McClain had been forbidden by Saundra from helping with the cleanup but he was not about to sit on his ass while everyone else worked. While Erik, Tyler, and Ortiz loaded bodies and body parts into the mule, McClain hobbled around on a crutch, needlessly supervising Saundra and Ashley as they nailed plywood and boards over the broken windows.

It took three trips with the mule to transport all the bodies to the church. Rather than line them up in neat rows as the women had done with their purloined corpses, Ortiz hauled them into the church and dumped them haphazardly into a pile on the floor behind the last row of pews.

On tables near the altar of the church, they found several mummified corpses wrapped in sheets that the women had not gotten around to washing and wrapping yet. In a smaller room in the basement there was a small stash of rifles, shotguns, and pistols, along with boxes of ammunition and open boxes of food and water.

"Must be their version of a man-cave," Tyler said to Ortiz. "Not as well stocked as yours though."

"This is whatever they scavenged from the surrounding houses," Ortiz said, picking through the random supplies. "No real long-term survival plan here."

"They probably intended to take over the mansion all along," Erik said. "Once they got you and McClain out of the way, they could claim the mansion and warehouse for themselves and be in a position to defend them too."

Ortiz nodded. "That could be what the men had in mind. The women probably just wanted to get rid of us demons so they could welcome the glorious return of their dear and fluffy lord."

"Shit," Tyler said. "Can you imagine what they could have done if they had gotten hold of your weapons and supplies? They could have taken over this whole city and turned it into an armed compound like... What was the name of that place in South America where all those cult members killed themselves?"

"Jonestown," Ortiz replied. "But I don't think this would have been any kind of religious compound. The women were pretty exclusive in their membership and single-minded in their beliefs. I have a feeling the men would have eventually decided they were going to be in charge. They probably planned to turn this little cult upside-down and force the women to be sex slaves or worse. It's been known to happen."

They loaded the guns and supplies into the mule to haul back to the mansion. Before leaving, Ortiz poured five gallons of motor oil throughout the inside of the church and out the door. He lit a match and they watched the church burn for twenty or thirty minutes before turning to head back to the mansion.

"Too bad there are no buzzards around," Ortiz said as they left the blaze behind them. "I would rather have left the bodies out in the open. I think the birds would have enjoyed the fresh meat."

Back at the mansion, they cleaned up the rest of the debris from the yard and spent the remainder of the day helping Saundra and Ashley with boarding up the windows.

Erik and Tyler were stripping boards off the pool shed in the back yard when Tyler casually asked, "So what was the big discussion last night all about?"

Erik was pretty sure what he was referring to but played ignorant anyway.

"What discussion?"

Tyler took a break from prying a board loose and looked at him. "You and Ashley. On the balcony last night? I had to get up to take a piss and I saw you two out there talking."

"Oh that. Yeah, we were just talking."

"I know that, dim-weed. But I can't figure it out. Here, I can't get her to say two words to me, and then I see you two on the balcony last night having what looked like some serious heart-to-heart discussion."

"She was just wondering how long we're planning on staying," Erik lied. "You know, when are we going to leave, are you leaving with me or staying here... that sort of stuff. I guess Saundra was wondering too."

"And she had to ask you that in the middle of the night? On the balcony?"

Erik shrugged. "I was up. So was she. I needed some fresh air and we didn't want to disturb anyone."

"Man, you lie about as well as I shoot." Tyler went back to prying at the boards with his hammer. "Only eligible girl left on the planet," he grumbled, "and a total babe to boot. It figures she would go for the Boy Scout on a crusade."

Erik tried suppressing a grin but failed. Seeing Tyler jealous over his talking with Ashley was entertaining but he felt it was all over nothing. He was pretty sure Ashley liked him as a friend and found him easy to talk to, but he seriously doubted she had any romantic interest in him. She had to be almost five years older than him. And since when did women ever go for younger guys? Sergeant Ortiz or Corporal McClain had a better chance with her than either he or Tyler, and he was putting his money on McClain.

At dinner that night, Saundra brought up the subject of their staying or leaving.

"Have you two decided if you're going to stay with us here and become part of our humble little family?" she asked. "Or are you still intent on going back into that horrible world out there?"

"Not that she's trying to guilt-trip you or anything," McClain said, grinning.

"I thought you got this all sorted out last night," Tyler said, glancing between Erik and Ashley.

"I didn't say for sure," Erik said. "But I've been thinking a lot about it and I think I should probably get back on the road as soon as possible. I was thinking of heading out tomorrow morning."

"So soon?" Saundra asked.

"You're welcome to stay as long as you want," Ortiz said. "You've certainly proven your worth around here. We'd be glad to have you."

"I would love to stay," Erik said and meant it. "This place is more of a home than anything I'm going to find out there, and I appreciate your taking us in. But I don't think I could ever be comfortable here without knowing if my mom and sister are alright. Besides, every day I stay, it's going to be that much harder to leave."

"What about you?" McClain asked Tyler.

"While I haven't done as much soul searching over it as the night stalker here," Tyler said, "I have given it a little thought. I've been telling him all along that I was going to jump ship at the first sign of civilization and, well, here it is."

"But you're going with him," Ortiz concluded.

Tyler sighed. "Yeah, I guess we're sort of a team now. If I stay here, I'll always be wondering to myself whatever happened to that crazy bastard and his silly quest." He gave a quick glance to Saundra but she let it slide. "Besides, someone has to watch his ass while he's busy saving puppies and helping old ladies."

"Well, two people on the road are definitely safer than one," McClain said. "And I've got to say, as much as I'd like to see you boys stay, at least for a little while longer, I'm glad you're sticking together."

"If you're absolutely sure you have to leave tomorrow," Saundra said, "the least we can do is give you whatever help we can. Whatever you need to be safe out there, just ask and we'll do our best to make sure you have it. Ashley and I will make sure you have clean clothes, proper supplies, and enough food to give you a good start."

"And for the harsher realities of the world," Ortiz said, "first thing tomorrow morning, meet us down in the rec room. We'll make sure that if anyone wants to mess with you out there, you can give them something else to think about."

***

Erik took the time to fully enjoy the feel of the mattress under him, the clean sheets and warm blankets over him, and the soft pillow under his head. After tonight, it would be back to sleeping along the side of the road, in old barns, or on the floor or couch of some stranger's living room. If they were lucky, they might find a house that had been unoccupied at the time of the storm and they would be able to spend the night in a real bed again, but those times were pretty hit or miss and always far between.

Tyler came in from using the bathroom, turned the flame on the lantern down, and flopped onto his bed with an exaggerated groan.

"Shit. I'm going to miss this bed. Do you think we can take it with us? If we like put wheels on it and tie a rope to it?"

Erik had to smile, envisioning them dragging a bed behind them down the middle of the interstate all the way to Iowa. It was like something out of a Monty Python skit.

"Yeah, sure. We'd probably make pretty good time too. One of us could sleep while the other pulls. We'll take shifts and go twenty-four hours a day."

"Sounds good to me. Except for the part where I have to drag *your* ass down the road."

Erik put his hands behind his head and stared up at the flickering shadows on the ceiling being thrown off by the lantern. After a while he asked, "So what made you decide civilization wasn't for you anymore?"

"You mean why I decided to go with you instead of staying here in a nice safe house with hot meals, hot water, and this comfy, warm bed?"

"Yeah. Ever since we left Aitkin, you've been pretty intent on finding a place to stay. Well, here it is, and I won't be in your way when Ashley finally succumbs to your witty charm and gentlemanly ways."

"What? You don't want me tagging along with you?" He switched to an annoyingly whiny voice. "Are you saying you don't *like* me anymore?"

"Get bent. You know what I mean."

Tyler was quiet for a few seconds before speaking again.

"Maybe it's that whole life-debt thing. You saved my life back there so now you're stuck with me until I save yours."

"That's bullshit and you know it. Sure, you were in danger of becoming an alcoholic. Big whoop. My grandmother was both an alcoholic and a chain-smoker and she lived to be eighty-two."

"Well, okay then, maybe it's because you're on some hero's quest like Frodo in *The Lord of the Rings* and you need a Samwise with you to keep your ass out of trouble."

"Samwise should have been the one carrying the ring. I always figured he could have gotten that ring to Mount Doom all on his own without Frodo stumbling along and getting them into trouble at every turn."

"Yeah, well, I guess that's why I'm Samwise The Strong and you're Frodo The Fuckup."

Erik laughed. "Up yours."

"Do you really think I could win Ashley over if I stayed?"

"I think you'd have a better chance with Saundra."

"Oh god! Now I have to picture that."

Tyler was quiet for a while before speaking again.

"I think it's just that life on the road these days is more interesting than sitting in one place. I mean, it's pretty obvious things aren't going to get better any time soon, so why not wander the roads and highways and see what's out there. Maybe we'll find some bigger community, or maybe there's someplace out there that got completely missed by the storm. If there is, I sure as hell won't find it hanging around this place."

Erik considered that. It made sense. Even if he didn't have a sister or family to go home to, traveling the roads seemed a better short-term plan than plunking down in one spot for the rest of his life. Sure, stay a day or two here, stay a few days there, but keep on the move and learn what's out there before deciding to call someplace home.

"Okay," he said, "but what about after we get to Iowa? Say I find my sister and we hang out at my house for a few days, assuming I let you in the door. What then? Do we stay there? Do we hit the road again? Or do we lay claim to the town and start our own survivor community?"

"I don't know. Nowadays, I don't see the sense in planning much beyond tomorrow. Maybe we wait and figure it out when we get there."

"Yeah." Erik sighed, still staring at the ceiling. He had been thinking about it almost every day the past week or so. Once he got home, then what? He had to believe that Sam was still alive and waiting for him – he couldn't bring himself to imagine otherwise. Could they stay at their house for long? It was a small town. If there were any other survivors, the supplies wouldn't last long. He figured maybe they would try to stay in the house at least for the winter. Then, maybe in the spring, move to the outskirts of a larger city.

But now, knowing about this place, with Saundra and Ashley and the soldiers – maybe they should come back up here. This was a good place with good people. Sam would like it here.

Erik closed his eyes and imagined Sam running down the wide halls of the mansion, playing hide and seek in its many rooms, exploring the cavernous attic, and using the crow's nest as a playhouse.

He smiled as he drifted off to sleep.

***

"You'll never find me," Sam called back over her shoulder as she ran down the hallway. Her blonde hair trailed after her as if in a strong wind. She turned abruptly and disappeared into one of the bedrooms.

Erik followed after her at a walk, letting her get well ahead of him and giving her time to hide. It was mid-afternoon in the springtime and sunlight was streaming in through the windows. The storm was long ago and long forgotten. He felt the fresh, warm breeze blowing in through the open windows. There was nothing to do all day but play games with Sam as she explored the mansion.

He reached the room she had darted into and paused before going in, giving her time to have heard his footsteps and freeze wherever she was hiding, still as a mouse. He guessed she was hiding in the armoire on the far side of the room. He would swing open both doors as fast as he could and shout, "Ah-ha!" And she would scream and laugh as he reached in and tickled her.

He stepped into the room but now it was no longer a bedroom with a big, antique armoire and king-size bed with a down comforter. Now he was in a forest, walking beneath the trees. Leaves and sticks crunched under his feet while sunlight dappled the ground through the branches above. Up ahead, he could see a break in the trees. A golden, rolling meadow filled with wildflowers of every color lay beyond.

Erik made his way to the clearing and stood looking out over the meadow. Above him, the sky was a fairy blue with wispy, white clouds drifting on a high breeze. Butterflies and dragonflies darted among the wildflowers and tall grass of the meadow. Bumblebees scoured the petals of goldenrod for nectar while goldfinches perched on the purple heads of thistles, digging for the seeds.

He walked out into the meadow, trailing his hands through the grasses and flowers, feeling them brush against his palms and between his fingers. The butterflies and dragonflies swirled in the air around him. The bumblebees ignored him while the goldfinches took flight, only to land again a few yards away and resume their hunt for thistle seeds.

He lay down on his back in the grass on a small hillock in the middle of the clearing and closed his eyes, feeling the warmth of the sun on his face. He forgot about the storm and the dead world it had left in its wake. Here, everything was alive and wonderful, the way it was supposed to be. He would stay in the meadow for a little while and then he would go and find Sam and bring her back here. This is where she belonged. This is the life she deserved.

He opened his eyes and saw butterflies flitting overhead on broad, bright, multicolored wings. He smiled as one dropped to his forehead, its legs and feelers tickling his brow ever so lightly. The butterfly flitted down to his nose and then to his lips, tickling him with each brush of its legs, each beat of its wings.

Erik opened his eyes. Ashley smiled, her face inches above his. He was in his bed and she was under the covers with him, lying lightly on top of him. He could hear Tyler's snores from his own bed across the room. Soft, flickering light was coming from the lantern on the dresser near the door.

Before he could say anything, Ashley placed a finger on his lips and planted another soft kiss on his nose. She moved to his mouth and kissed him more firmly, her lips lingering on his. He was woefully lacking in experience but he kissed her back as best he could, copying her technique, letting her be his teacher. He felt her tongue flick between his lips. He wrapped his arms around her and felt the bare skin of her lower back. Suddenly, his heart was racing.

She kissed him deeper, more passionately now. She stopped only long enough to slide his underwear off as she moved to straddle his hips. Leaning forward, she smiled and kissed him again, at the same time reaching down and guiding him into her.

She pushed herself up. In the flickering light of the candle, Erik could see her breasts, her throat, and her hair shining in the light of the lantern. She took his hands and placed them on her breasts. She closed her eyes and began slowly rocking her pelvis against his.

He was in too much pleasure to think of what to do. This absolutely had to be a dream, but he went with it. His hands explored her body, caressing her breasts and then down her sides to her stomach, her hips, her thighs, feeling her muscles tense and flex as she moved on top of him.

She leaned forward and he took one of her breasts in his mouth, sucking lightly on her nipple. She gave a light gasp and began thrusting faster, more forcefully, pushing him deeper into her.

He closed his eyes and let his hands slide down her body to her hips. He gripped her tightly, pulling her closer, losing himself to the pleasure.

He began to respond to her thrusts with his own, matching her increasing rhythm. Too soon, he felt the rush of orgasm and then nothing else in the world mattered.

She stopped, letting him finish, and then began rocking her hips in long, slow thrusts. Soon her rhythm began to speed up again and she thrust against him harder, her breath coming in short gasps. And then, suddenly, her whole body tensed. She threw her head back and drew in a sharp breath. Her hips clamped down on him like a warm vise, pushing him into her as deep as she could.

He wrapped his arms around her waist and held her to him. Soon her body relaxed. She made a small sound like a pleasant sigh and looked down at him, smiling, her eyes half closed.

She leaned forward and lay on top of him, resting her head on his chest.

Erik felt completely drained. With as much effort as he could summon, he wrapped his arms around her and held her to him, not wanting this dream to end. He buried his face in her hair and breathed deep, savoring every bit of her.

They lay together for a long time, catching their breaths, letting blood return to vital organs. Erik gently caressed her back as she slowly trailed her fingertips lightly up and down the side of his face, around his ear, and then down his neck and shoulder.

When Ashley lifted herself up, she once again smiled and placed a finger to his lips. She slid off him and planted one last, soft kiss on his mouth before slipping off the bed.

Erik rolled his head to the side to look for her but she was already gone, the door easing closed behind her.

He lay there in the darkness, too spent to move and too blissful to care. After a few minutes, he again grew aware of Tyler's snoring from across the room. He lay there, still seeing Ashley's face and body in the soft shadows of the lantern flame, feeling her breasts under his hands, feeling her weight on top of him, feeling himself inside her. He played it over and over again in his head until the memory slipped quietly into his dreams.

JULY 13

"But why are *you* going?" Saundra asked Tyler. "You're from Minnesota. Why would you go to Iowa? What will you do there?"

Erik and Tyler were sitting at the kitchen table, finishing up Saundra's breakfast of pancakes with maple syrup and slices of fried Spam, which never seemed to go bad, even in the apocalypse.

"I'm Samwise," Tyler said. "Without Samwise, Frodo can't make it to Mount Doom. He can't complete his quest."

Saundra looked perplexed. "Who's Frodo?"

"He's Frodo," Tyler said, gesturing to Erik. "Sure, he's kind of a bumbling dork and he should give the ring to me and go home, but that's not the way the story's written."

Saundra turned to Erik. "Do you know what he's talking about?"

"What?" Erik asked. He looked up, not sure what either of them had been talking about. He'd been putting food into his mouth and chewing without thinking about it while replaying the events of last night over and over in his head. Now, he wasn't sure if any of it was real. He was beginning to think it was nothing more than some amazing, wonderful dream.

"*The Lord of the Rings*," Tyler said. "You've never read it or seen the movies?"

"Oh yes!" Saundra said. "*The Lord of the Rings*. I've heard of it."

"But you don't know who Frodo and Samwise are?"

"Well, no. I've heard of it but I've never read it. And I never had much time for motion pictures. I did read *Lord of the Flies* when I was a young woman in college. Goodness, but that was a long time ago! But I don't remember any of the characters except Piggy. They treated him so awful in the book."

Tyler threw his hands up. "Oh my god! We have a heathen among us." He shook his head sadly and then asked, "What about Don Quixote and Poncho Sanchez?"

"Oh yes, I've heard of them. That story's a classic."

"Okay then. He's Don Quixote," Tyler said, pointing at Erik. He then pointed his thumb back to himself. "I'm Poncho Sanchez."

"But wasn't Don Quixote crazy?" Saundra asked.

Tyler dropped his head to the table and groaned.

Saundra leaned toward Erik and whispered conspiratorially, "I'm just messing with him."

Erik stared at her blankly.

She reached across the table and placed the back of her hand to his forehead and then his cheek.

"Are you feeling alright? You look a little under the weather. Maybe you should stay here another day."

"Good morning!" Ashley walked into the kitchen. She crossed quickly to the cupboard and opened it, rummaging through the boxes of dry breakfast cereal. She glanced over her shoulder to the three sitting at the table. "What's going on here? What did I miss?"

Tyler raised his head. "We have a heathen in our midst."

"I was asking Erik how he felt," Saundra said. "He looks tired this morning. I hope he's not coming down with something."

"Who's the heathen?" Ashley asked. She sat down at the table and poured some frosted flakes into a bowl. She pulled her feet up under her and began picking flakes out of the bowl one at a time and popping them into her mouth.

"Do you know who Frodo and Samwise are?" Tyler asked her.

"Of course. Doesn't everyone?"

Tyler stabbed his finger at Saundra.

"Do you want some water?" Saundra asked Erik.

"I'm fine," Erik said. "I don't think I got enough sleep last night. I had some weird dreams." He stole a glance toward Ashley.

Ashley looked back at him, still munching on her cereal. She raised her eyebrows in a curious expression.

"Really? What about?"

Erik sighed and glanced back down at the table. "Doesn't matter. Maybe I'm losing my mind."

Ortiz came into the room and rapped his knuckles on the table. "Hey! If you guys are hitting the road this morning, let's get you stocked up. Grab your packs and follow me."

As they followed him out of the room, Erik cast a quick glance back to the kitchen. Saundra and Ashley were discussing something. Neither glanced back to him. Of course, it had to have been a dream.

McClain was waiting for them in the rec room, on his feet but leaning back against a padded recliner and his crutch under one arm. He swept his other arm to take in the whole room.

"The candy store is open, boys. Take anything you like. I'm serious. If it hadn't been for your help the other night, we might not even be here."

"Let me make a couple of suggestions," Ortiz said. He picked up two canvas pistol belts with holsters and handed one each to Erik and Tyler. The bullet loops around each belt were full. "I took the liberty of filling these with forty-five and forty-four caliber rounds last night. You've each got thirty shots there. Grab a couple more boxes and whatever you think you can carry."

"And put your pistols in those belts," McClain said. "Don't keep them in your backpacks. If you need them, you're going to need them right goddamn now. By the time you dig them out of your packs, it will be too late and you'll be dead."

As they strapped on the belts, McClain nodded to a wooden crate on the floor.

"Before you fill you packs too full, reach in there and take a bottle each."

Tyler opened the crate and pulled out a brown bottle. He looked at the label and then handed it to Erik.

"Twenty-five-year-old single-barrel Canadian rye whiskey," McClain said. "Found that in the cellar of one of these other houses here. Back when money was worth something, that stuff would have gone for near seventy or eighty bucks a bottle, maybe more."

Tyler pulled another bottle out and studied it. "Is it good?"

"I think it's the nectar of the gods," McClain said. "But that's me. It's special and very rare, especially nowadays. Of course, if you don't like it, you can always use it to barter for something else you need."

"Food, women, guns… the necessities," Ortiz said with a wink, "but not necessarily in that order."

Erik and Tyler put the bottles into their backpacks and then set about packing as much food, water, and whatever else that looked like it might be helpful on the road. Erik noticed that, in addition to a change of clean clothes, Saundra had also packed them each a small first aid kit.

Ortiz picked up a small twenty-two caliber lever-action rifle. "Here. You should probably take this too. Nothing better for taking down small game if you need to. It will also take down larger game like deer if your aim is good enough. And it breaks down for easy carrying." He twisted a thumbscrew on the side and separated the rifle into two halves to demonstrate.

"And if it comes to it," McClain added, "it works pretty good as a sniper weapon. Quiet. Accurate. I've already sighted it in for you. It's dead-on at one hundred yards."

Erik took the rifle and slid the two halves into the side loops of his backpack and then added a box of shells for it.

Their packs were fairly bursting and weighing upwards of thirty pounds now. Shrugging them onto their shoulders, Erik and Tyler went back upstairs. Everyone in the mansion joined them on the front porch to see them off and wish them luck.

"You boys will do well," Ortiz said, shaking their hands. "If you can handle yourself on the road half as well as you handled yourselves the other night, you won't have any problems."

"Other than a hernia from this damn pack," Tyler grumbled.

"You'll get used to it. By the time you get to Iowa, you'll be so strong you won't even notice them anymore."

"Stick together and watch each other's back," McClain said. "Stay low and be wary of people you meet. As an old friend of mine from basic training used to say, trust no one, suspect everyone."

"Oh hush," Saundra said, already dabbing a handkerchief to her eyes. "What kind of attitude is that?"

"In these times, one that just might save their lives."

Saundra hugged them both and kissed each one on the cheek.

"God be with both of you. I'll be praying for you. If it gets too difficult or dangerous out there, or for any reason at all, please, please come on back. You know you're always welcome here." She stepped back and smiled at them, dabbing at her eyes again.

"That goes for me too," Ortiz said. "Seriously, you've made it this far on just your wits and that shows you've got good instincts. But if you run into trouble, if you find you can't move forward for some reason, remember you can always come back."

"If we have to bug out of this place for any reason," McClain said, "we'll leave a note of some kind. Probably carve it right on the door here. You won't miss it."

"Anything but red paint," Erik suggested.

Ashley was last. She hugged Tyler and wished him luck. She then put her mouth close to his ear and whispered something. She gave him a peck on the cheek and stepped back, locking her gaze on his as if driving home some point. Tyler's eyebrows were raised a bit and he looked perplexed.

She then turned to Erik with a mischievous smile.

"Weird dream, huh? If you're ever back this way, we're going to have to get together and have a talk about that."

Before Erik could say anything, she stepped forward and wrapped her arms around him, putting her head over his shoulder and hugging him tight. As he hugged her back, she turned her head and brushed her lips against his ear, whispering, "Thank you for being a friend."

Taking his face in her hands, she touched her lips to his and kissed him softly at first and then more passionately. He responded, pulling her closer and becoming oblivious to everything else around them. For now, there was only Ashley and the passion in her kiss. He didn't know how long it lasted before she pulled back and smiled at him but it wasn't long enough.

"Go on, hero," she said. "Sam is waiting. Keep your promise. Do what you have to do, but always remember we're here for you. *I'm* here for you."

He wanted to promise her he would be back. But he had another promise to keep first.

As Ashley stepped back, he became aware that everyone was looking at him. Saundra had a slightly embarrassed expression. Ortiz and McClain were both grinning. Tyler was looking at him as though he had suddenly grown another head and two more arms.

"Good luck," Ortiz said. "And remember, watch each other's backs."

Everyone said one final goodbye, with Saundra again commanding God to bless and protect them. Erik and Tyler then shouldered their packs and headed down the driveway. They stopped once at the gate to turn and wave and then started up the road, heading back to the highway to resume their trek south.

Erik was feeling mixed emotions about leaving. Part of him told himself that leaving was stupid. Here was a place of safety. Here was comfort, shelter, and friends. But Sam was still in Iowa, waiting for him. And that part of himself Ashley called the hero – whether it was true or not – overrode everything else. Even if he had not made that promise to Sam, nothing would stop him from going back for her. Nothing would stop him from trying.

Neither spoke until they reached the intersection of the highway. Erik glanced back once but they had already passed beyond sight of the mansion.

"So...," Tyler said. "What in hell was that all about?"

"What was what all about?"

"You know damn well what. Ashley. What in the hell is between you two?"

Erik shrugged, feigning ignorance. "Nothing. She was just saying goodbye."

"Bullshit, you fucking liar. I didn't get a goodbye like that. She didn't shove her tongue down *my* throat. Hell, I thought you two were going to rip each other's clothes off and go at it right there in front of everyone."

Erik laughed. "We're just friends."

"Friends don't try to swallow each other's faces. 'I'm here for you?' You know what she said to me? She said I'd better watch your back and not let anything happen to you or she'd hunt me down and roast my balls on a sharp stick over a low fire."

Erik laughed again and shook his head. "Don't think she wouldn't do it." He started walking again.

"And what was that crack about weird dreams?" Tyler asked, catching up with him. "Something happened between you two and I'm pretty damn sure I know what it was."

"Well, if you know, then I guess I don't have to tell you."

"Tell me anyway."

"Maybe," Erik said. "Maybe after the next apocalypse."

***

They followed the highway south for the rest of the day. The extra weight of their backpacks forced them to take more frequent rest breaks than usual but Erik figured they were still making good time.

As they approached Minneapolis, they saw what Ashley had described to Corporal McClain. An enormous black cloud hung low and menacing over the entire city. Dozens of columns of smoke, maybe hundreds, were still feeding it.

"Damn," Tyler said. "The whole city's burning. And there are still survivors there? Gangs? Don't they know that without any wind, that smoke is going to sit there and eventually choke them all to death?"

"It's the end of the world," Erik said. "I suppose most of them have either already fled the city or they just don't care."

Tyler shook his head. "Fucking crazy. It they're too stupid to leave, it's probably better that they choke to death."

Nearing evening, they passed the burned-out hulk of a passenger plane lying in a field off to their right. Several crows were investigating the wreckage. A single coyote was trotting back and forth through the debris, sniffing and pawing at the ground around the crumpled hunks of blackened metal.

"Think they're eating the bodies?" Tyler asked.

"Probably. Nature's clean-up crew in action. It might not be pretty but at least we're starting to see more life."

Not far past the wreckage of the plane, they came to a highway overpass with a tractor-trailer rig dangling precariously over the edge. They set up camp on the embankment under the bridge, keeping far enough to the opposite side so if the truck fell during the night, they wouldn't end up as roadkill.

They built a small campfire to heat their food, wary of how far away someone would be able to see the light in the darkness. Any wanderers that came upon them would likely be coming from the ruins of Minneapolis, and Erik hoped the overpass and embankments would give them adequate concealment.

After they'd eaten and as they lay back on the embankment, Erik became aware of the low, distant thrumming of bullfrogs. This was the first time he had heard frogs since the storm. Closing his eyes, he listened to them and felt for the first time that maybe things were going to be okay.

He had begun to doze off, imagining a future where the sky was clear again and the sun was shining down on lush, green meadows and trees bursting with leaves, when Tyler's voice suddenly jarred him back to reality.

"You think those astronauts are still alive?"

He hesitated, having to think about what Tyler was asking.

"What in the hell are you talking about?"

"The space station. It's probably still up there, right? And they keep months' worth of supplies on board."

"Jeeze, I don't know."

Tyler was quiet for about a minute before speaking again.

"That would suck, man. You know? If they're still alive up there, how in hell will they ever get back?"

"Jump," Erik said, closing his eyes again. "Just open the airlock and step out. Beats starving to death in a floating tin can." He listened for the frogs again but they seemed to have stopped for the night.

Tyler fell silent again for a while. Erik began to doze again, this time his thoughts on Ashley and her surprise visit to his bed last night, which he was glad to know had *not* been a dream after all.

Tyler's voice jarred him awake again.

"I bet people in submarines survived. If it didn't kill the fish, that means everyone who was under the water is probably alive too, right?"

Erik said nothing, didn't move, hoping Tyler would take the hint and shut up and go to sleep.

"I wonder what they thought," Tyler continued. "All those sailors, when they surfaced and came into port. I bet they were all like, 'What the hell? Was there a war and nobody invited us?'"

Erik remained silent, still playing possum. After a couple of minutes, he was thinking his ruse had worked. But then…

"You and Ashley had sex, didn't you?"

"Jesus! Would you go to sleep already?"

Tyler laughed. "Ha! Knew you were faking it."

"I'm just trying to get some sleep."

"Why? Did you have a long night last night? Did that 'weird dream' keep you awake?"

"If you don't shut up and go to sleep, I'm going to go up and push that damn semi down on top of you."

"You must have gone to her room. Or did you do it somewhere else? Had to be somewhere no one would walk in on you."

Erik was about to tell him it was none of his damn business when he heard the faint strains of music coming from somewhere far away. He sat up and turned his head, trying to determine where it was coming from.

"What?" Tyler asked, also sitting up.

"Listen. What is that?"

Tyler listened for a few seconds. "Bagpipes!"

After a few bars, Erik thought he recognized the tune.

"Sounds like *Amazing Grace*."

"I think it is, yeah."

They sat there by the light of the small campfire for several minutes, listening to the slow, haunting melody drift from somewhere out of the darkness. It filled Erik with a kind of sad loneliness. It sounded as though someone was playing a funeral dirge for someone they had lost, or maybe for the whole world.

When the music ended, Erik lay back on the embankment and stared up at the flickering shadows on the concrete overpass above him. Tyler also lay back. Neither one said another word.

As he watched the play of light and shadow above, Erik thought of the music and of the attack at the mansion, of the dead bodies all over the ground, and the growing black cloud over Minneapolis. He thought of Crazy Bob and how he'd had to shoot him. He thought of Seth, buried in an unmarked grave in some unknown horse pasture a hundred miles north of here. Finally, he thought of all the people and things he would never see again, things he would never do again.

His earlier feeling that things were going to be okay was naive. It was only the beginning of this new world, and it was cold and dark and lonely, full of death and sadness and danger.

How could anything ever be okay again?

JULY 16

Three days after leaving the mansion at Elk River, Erik and Tyler had put at least fifty miles between themselves and the massive black cloud hanging over Minneapolis. They had stuck to highway 169 and skirted along the western suburbs of the city, staying in houses all along the way after that first night under the overpass. Tyler was right. The whole city was one suburb after another. There was no shortage of houses to stay in or stores to scavenge for food and supplies.

Here and there they passed a tree that still had green leaves on it and the occasional patch of green in a field of brown. They had also seen a few more animals – a few birds, two or three squirrels, rabbits, and two small, fluffy white dogs playing in the backyard of a house. Erik wasn't sure if more life had survived farther south or if they were seeing more survivors because they were covering more ground every day.

On the afternoon of the third day, they detoured off the highway to a small community of scattered houses and a few neighborhood stores. They found a small grocery store and went in, looking to top off their supplies, only to find the store had been looted of nearly everything.

"This crap again?" Tyler asked disgustedly. "What is with everyone hoarding shit? Christ, just take what you need and leave the rest. Other people are trying to survive too."

"People panic," Erik said. "Or they're trying to make sure they have enough to survive for a while. Hell, you were doing the same thing when Seth and I found you. And remember the rec room at the mansion?"

"Sure, fine, whatever. But at this rate, we're eventually going to be forced to join some survivor group, like back at the mansion. Everything will be scavenged out or hoarded by someone else."

"Yeah, but when some groups start running low on supplies and they see other groups with more than enough, there's going to be a lot more of what we saw back in Elk River. I think maybe we're in the calm between storms right now."

They left the store and continued along the road toward a group of houses. They approached the first one and saw the front door had been kicked in.

"What do you think?" Erik asked.

"Well, there's no cross on it. But we also know there's someone in town here hoarding supplies." Tyler looked around at the neighboring houses. "We could try another one but I'm seeing a couple of broken windows and at least one other door kicked in. My gut's telling me whatever we find or don't find in this house, all the others are going to be exactly the same."

"Might as well see what we're up against," Erik agreed.

Erring on the side of caution, he drew his pistol from its holster. Tyler did the same and they cautiously approached the house.

Inside, the house looked like every other home they'd been in, as though the owners had stepped out for a bit and could be back at any time. But when they reached the kitchen, they both stopped and stared in shock.

There was blood everywhere – on the counters, on the walls, on the refrigerator, and a large, smeared pool on the floor. The blood had dried and turned black. Off to the side of the pool lay a large kitchen knife like the one the old woman had attacked him with. The blade was black with blood. A thick smear on the floor led out a doorway that was open to the hallway on the other side of the kitchen.

Erik and Tyler looked at each other. Tyler motioned with his hand that Erik should follow the smear while he went around to the hallway through the other room. Erik nodded.

As Tyler backed out of the kitchen, Erik carefully cocked his pistol and held it ready, cautiously stepping around the blood and across the kitchen to the doorway on the other side. The smear disappeared into the hall. He stepped up to the doorway, took a deep breath, and then slowly peered around the corner.

A body was lying face down in the hallway a few feet away. It appeared to be a teenage boy. The off-white carpet in the hall was stained black all around the body. Erik glanced to his right and saw Tyler enter the hallway from the living room. Erik pointed to the body and then stepped around it. He moved farther down the hall, checking each room as Tyler followed.

In the first bedroom, the body of a girl lay naked on the bed. She hadn't been mummified and she couldn't have been more than twelve or thirteen years old. She was lying on her back, arms and legs spread-eagle across the bed. She had been raped and her throat had been slit.

"Jesus," Erik moaned and quickly turned away. He felt his stomach knotting up. It was all he could do to keep from vomiting. He leaned back against the wall and motioned for Tyler to check the master bedroom.

Tyler moved past him, glancing into the room and then quickly looking away. He moved to the master bedroom and stared into it for a couple of seconds before turning back to Erik.

"Same thing," he whispered. "Mother's been raped and murdered. Don't see anyone else."

Erik put his head back against the wall and squeezed his eyes shut. Too many thoughts and emotions were swirling inside of him. He couldn't concentrate, couldn't think. He felt himself filling with a deep anger and loathing, rage for whoever had done this.

He took several deep breaths and let them out slowly, trying to keep his feelings from exploding out of him. When he opened his eyes, he saw Tyler investigating the body of the boy in the hall.

Tyler rolled the body onto its side, examined it, and then rolled the boy back onto his stomach again.

"I bet he's the brother. He's been shot and gutted." He glanced back to the kitchen. "I bet he tried to defend them with that knife."

"Jesus," Erik said. "What kind of fucking animals would do this?"

Tyler had no answers. "What do you want to do?" he asked.

"You mean other than track down the bastards that did this and skin them alive?" Erik shook his head. "I don't know."

He felt the rage boiling up inside again. He abruptly turned and strode quickly down the hallway, pushing past Tyler, and then through the living room and out the front door. He stood on the front steps, looking up and down the street, and then he raised his face to the overcast sky and let out all his frustration and rage in one long and loud scream.

When his rage was exhausted, he sat down heavily on the front steps. He stared out across the street at nothing for several minutes. Thoughts of Sam kept filling his head and of what she could be facing if she was still alive and alone. He looked down and closed his eyes, trying to push the thoughts away. He wanted to be home now, *right now*, and his frustration began to grow again, like a balloon inside of him ready to burst his body apart.

The pistol fell from his hand and he heard it clatter on the sidewalk. He covered his face with his hands and cried into them. For the first time since the storm, he contemplated that Sam might not have survived. He thought that maybe it would be for the best, if the storm had taken her, and he hated himself for thinking it. He cried into his hands and heard someone sobbing, "I'm sorry," over and over again. After a while, he realized it was himself.

When he finally looked up, he saw Tyler sitting on the steps beside him. It was darker now, almost evening. He didn't know how long he had been sitting there but it must have been at least an hour.

"I covered the bodies," Tyler said. "I put them all together in the mother's bed and covered them with fresh blankets. That's the best we can do for them."

Erik let out a deep, shuddering sigh. He had never felt so empty, so defeated, so helpless in all his life. He picked up his pistol and got slowly to his feet.

"Come on," he said, putting the pistol back into its holster. "Let's get the fuck out of here."

***

They walked in silence for over an hour, heading south on the same street. Erik didn't think anything, didn't feel anything. For now, he just wanted to keep moving, keep walking and never stop. He stared down at the road immediately ahead of himself, putting one foot ahead of the other and ignoring everything else.

It was the change in the road that brought him back to awareness of his surroundings. The hard pavement had given way to crushed gravel. He stopped and glanced around, surprised that full darkness was almost upon them.

They were on a straight, gravel road that disappeared into the woods after about a mile. Up ahead and to their right was a narrow, dirt driveway leading from the road to a small, ramshackle farmhouse and rusty pickup truck sitting alone in the center of a patch of tall, dead grass. A cornfield encircled the small homestead on three sides. Along the left side of the road was another cornfield and then a stretch of dead woods.

He turned and looked back. The small community they had come through was nowhere in sight. There was only the road coming from the north with cornfields, a few groves of trees on either side, and a pasture off to the east.

"Where the hell are we?" he asked.

"I don't know, man," Tyler said. "You were walking and I was following. I didn't know if you were going to stop or keep going until morning."

Erik turned again and looked at the little farmhouse. As he did, the front door opened and a big, yellow dog came bounding out. It jumped off the porch and loped up the driveway towards them, its tail wagging and its tongue hanging out. A tall, rail-thin black man in bib overalls and flannel shirt stepped out of the lighted doorway of the farmhouse and onto the porch. He held a double-barreled shotgun in his hands but it was down at his waist and pointed off to the side.

The dog reached the end of the driveway. It was a golden retriever and it was happy to meet them, bouncing in circles around them and wagging its tail so forcefully its whole body twisted from side to side. Every now and then it would let out a single enthusiastic bark.

Tyler crouched down and wrapped his arms around its neck, hugging the dog to his chest. He dug his fingers into its thick fur and scratched it furiously as it licked his face.

"Yes, yes," Tyler laughed, turning his face from side to side, trying to avoid the dog's rapid-fire tongue. "I missed you too, whoever you are."

Erik also crouched down and became a target of the happy tongue. He scratched the retriever behind the ears and down the neck.

The man on the porch gave a sharp whistle.

"Cyrano! You come on inside now. And bring your new friends with you."

The dog turned and bounded back up the driveway, circling back to the boys twice to make sure they were still following. On the porch, it circled the man once and then sat down on its haunches next to him, still whipping its tail back and forth, panting, and watching the boys' approach. The man switched his shotgun to one hand and used the other to reach down and scratch the top of the dog's head.

"It's near dark," the man said as Erik and Tyler approached the porch. "You boys best come on inside. You don't want to be on the road at night."

From the light coming through the doorway, Erik could see he was about seventy years old, with a wreath of short, white hair encircling his otherwise bald head. Deep wrinkles creased his face from years in the wind and sun. About a weeks' worth of white stubble covered his chin.

"We were passing on the road and saw your dog," Tyler offered in some way of a greeting. "We weren't looking to bother you."

"Don't know where you would be passin' to," the old man said. "That road there goes nowhere. Dead ends at the river a couple miles down in those woods."

"Yeah, we kind of got off track," Erik said. "We're heading south and got off the highway for a bit."

"Well, you boys come on inside. I was just gettin' ready to heat up some supper. You're welcome to join me. Name's Red, by the way. This is Cyrano."

The boys shook his hand and introduced themselves as they filed into the house.

The farmhouse was small and had only three or four rooms, but it was clean and comfortable, with a small table and chairs, a couch, and a wooden rocking chair in the main room. A small fire was burning in the fireplace. Cyrano trotted over to the rug in front of the fire, turned around twice, and then lay down, planting his head between his paws so he could watch everyone.

Erik noticed how Red cocked an eye at the guns in their belts.

"We're not scavengers or survivalists or anything like that," Erik said. "We just carry these for protection on the road."

"Of course, you're scavengers," Red said, closing the door. He leaned his shotgun against the wall. "We all are now. And I don't believe you intend any trouble. Cyrano there vouched for ya and I trust his instincts. But I was thinkin' that's some mighty big hardware you boys are carryin'."

"They were gifts," Erik said. "A man up in Garrison gave them to us. He was worried about the kinds of people we might meet on the road."

"Garrison! You boys *have* been on the road a while. Drop those packs anywhere and take a seat. I'll fix ya somethin' hot to eat and you can tell me about it."

As Red went into the kitchen, which was not much more than an extension of the combined dining and living rooms, Erik and Tyler leaned their backpacks against the wall next to the shotgun and hung their pistol belts on wooden hooks. They each took a seat at the small table. Cyrano watched them from his rug by the fire.

Red returned with a dusty wine bottle and three tin cups. He placed a cup in front of each of them and took a seat in the third chair.

"Got some stew heating up on the stove. Canned, of course. Can't find much in the way of fresh stuff anymore." He uncorked the bottle and poured a little of the rose-colored wine into each of the cups. "Sorry about the tin cups. Ain't no proper way to drink mead, but my hands shake from time to time and I've broken all my drinking glasses."

Tyler picked up his cup and sniffed at the contents. "Mead?"

"Honey wine." Red raised his own cup in a kind of toast. "This here's made with cherries so it's a bit more mellow than the straight stuff." He took a sip.

Erik and Tyler also raised their cups and sipped at the wine. Erik was surprised at the smooth, mellow flavor with a hint of cherry.

"This is really good!"

"Yup. Had a brother down in Iowa used to keep bees. He got tired of bottlin' the honey for sale, so he started turnin' it into mead. I've got maybe ten, twenty bottles around here somewhere. At least I think I do." He shook his head. "My memory ain't worth a spit anymore."

"It's very smooth," Tyler said, taking another sip.

"You go easy on it now. My brother makes it wicked strong. It's not your ordinary table wine. He adds the fruit to mellow it out but it also disguises the alcohol content. A few glasses of this and you'll be under the table talkin' to the dog, and he'll be talkin' back."

Red refilled their cups and then went back into the kitchen. He brought out three steaming bowls of stew and set them on the table. As they ate and sipped at the mead, the boys told him about their journey, from Erik's start north of Grand Rapids to the attack on the mansion in Elk River. The old man was genuinely surprised at how few survivors they had come across and especially troubled about the ongoing decline of Minneapolis.

"I don't stray too far from my house here anymore, so I don't see much of the world. But I get up to that little town up the road now and again. From what I seen there, I knew it was bad. But from what you boys are describin', it sounds a whole lot worse than anything I imagined."

"It's big," Tyler said. "With Minneapolis burning and crashed planes on the ground… It's been more than a month now and no one's come to investigate. It must be like this all over the country, probably all over the world."

"There was a doctor up at the mansion we stayed at," Erik said. "His guess was the other side of the world was entirely wiped out, and that radiation killed most everyone on this side."

Red shook his head and divided the last of the mead between the three cups.

"I don't envy you boys. I'm seventy-six years old, so I ain't got much longer anyways. But you boys, you're the ones who are gonna have to live through this and come out the other end, if there is an end."

He raised his cup and held it there until Erik and Tyler had raised there's.

"God be with you boys, whatever you perceive him to be."

***

They spread their sleeping bags out and joined Cyrano on Red's floor for the night. By the crackling light of the fire, and with the retriever's head resting on his stomach, Erik's doubts and frustrations began to ease a little.

He had always known what he might find when he got home, but he had always pushed it to the back of his mind. The horror he had seen in the little town up the road had dragged those fears out of their hiding place and shoved them right in his face, forcing him to acknowledge the likely truth.

In his thoughts of home, he had stubbornly pictured Sam as he'd always seen her, with her bright blue eyes and blonde hair, playing in the grass in the sun or curled up next to him as he read her a bedtime story. But that's not what he would find. Whatever he found when he got home, it certainly would not be that.

He stared at the dying fire while stroking Cyrano's fur. Red's mead was making his head buzz a bit. He had promised Sam he would come home and would keep that promise no matter what. If that wasn't good enough for Sister Angie's god or Saundra's god or anyone else's god, whatever they perceived him to be, then so be it. Wherever Sam was, she would know he had kept his promise. And that was all that mattered.

JULY 17

In the morning, Red fixed them a breakfast of oatmeal with cinnamon and honey. He added bread toasted over the gas stove, raspberry jam, and some fresh cantaloupe he'd found earlier in a garden that had survived the storm.

As they were preparing to leave, Red offered them each a bottle of his brother's mead. The boys tried to politely refuse but Red insisted.

"Go on, take it. I've got plenty more, much more than I'll ever get around to drinking at my age. It's too good to let sit around and turn to vinegar."

As they put the bottles in their packs, Erik took his bottle of rye whiskey from the mansion and handed it to Red.

"Thanks for letting us stay the night and for breakfast."

"We have it on good authority that this stuff is nectar of the gods," Tyler said.

Red took the bottle and squinted at the label. "Oh my, that it is!" He glanced back up at the boys. "Now, the polite thing for me to do is refuse to accept this."

"You can't," Erik said. "It's a gift. Besides, we've got another bottle."

"And we know where the source is," Tyler added.

Red grinned. "I was hopin' you'd say that. Thank you kindly indeed. It's been a long time since I've tasted good sippin' whiskey." He set the bottle aside and shook their hands. "You boys take care now. I know you're plenty-well armed and you seem able to take care of yourselves well enough, but you keep your heads up and your asses down. There was a group of three men that came through that town up there a few days ago and I think they were headin' south too. I don't know who they were but they didn't look like they was spreadin' the word o' the Lord, if you know what I mean."

"Three of them?" Erik asked.

"A big, tall fella, a fat one, and a smaller one. I stayed outa sight but I could see they was carryin' more hardware than one would need if they was huntin' rabbits and such. They didn't look like the kind of men who would give you a pass 'cause you're boys."

"We'll watch out for them," Tyler promised.

They said goodbye and thanked him again. The temperature had continued to fall gradually and it was chilly enough this morning they donned the light jackets Saundra had packed for them.

Cyrano accompanied them up the dirt lane to the gravel road, trotting alongside first one and then the other, collecting as many pets and head scratches as he could before Red's whistle called him back to the porch.

Once they reached the paved street again, they followed Red's directions back to the highway.

"You think it was those three Red told us about that murdered that family?" Tyler asked as they resumed their trek south on 169.

"It's got to be. Parasites like that, they're probably moving from town to town, taking what they want from whoever has it. They don't care about anyone but themselves."

"You're not thinking of trying to track them down, are you? You got kind of a scary look in your eyes when Red mentioned them."

"Yeah, I guess that was my first thought – track the bastards down and make them pay for what they did. But now..." He shook his head. "Now I say fuck 'em. Why waste our time or risk our lives on pieces of shit like that?"

"What are we going to do if we run across them?"

"I don't know. Maybe do like Red suggested and stay low and out of sight." Erik shrugged. "Doubtful we'll run into them anyway. They may be headed south too, but I think our chances of crossing paths with them are pretty slim."

By midday they had covered a little more than six miles. They stopped beneath a grove of trees in the median of the highway to eat lunch and to check the map, planning where they might be able to stop for the night.

"Eldeswold is up the road, maybe another six or seven miles," Erik said. "We should be able to make it there before dark."

"And if the three stooges are there?"

"Then we stay low and go around, I guess." Erik folded the map and put it back into his pack. "Too bad we didn't bring a couple of those M-16s from the mansion."

"You've got that rifle," Tyler said. "Could take them out from a distance. But then, do we really want to be picking fights? I mean, sure, maybe they deserve to die, but is it our job to be the policemen of the apocalypse?"

Erik thought about it, remembering the shoot-out at the mansion. They had gotten lucky there, with the soldiers' pre-planning and setting of the bombs. And yet Corporal McClain had still been shot and each of them had been wounded. Without the high-powered rifles and the booby-traps, things would have undoubtedly gone much worse.

"You're right," he said. "We'll avoid them if we can. I don't want to get into a running gun battle where we have to look over our shoulders all the way to Iowa. But if we can't avoid them, and things start looking bad, then I don't think we should hesitate for a second to take out all three of those rat-bastards before they can do the same to us."

Tyler nodded. "Go down swinging. I'm good with that."

They took inventory of their supplies and discovered they had far less food and water than expected, though they seemed fairly well-stocked in booze and bullets. They decided if the stores in Eldeswold were also looted, they would have to search houses until they were fully restocked. Towns and houses were getting farther and farther apart each day, so they would have to start being more mindful of their supplies.

The town turned out to be a little farther away than Erik estimated. They stopped for the night while they were still about a mile north of town, making camp inside the woods off the road in another creek bed. This one had run dry from lack of rain.

They built a small fire and heated up some baked beans and vegetable soup, which was pretty much the last of their supplies for the road, save for some beef jerky and granola bars. Erik pulled out the bottle of peach brandy and looked at how much was left – a little less than half.

"Might as well finish this off," he said. "Make room for whatever we can find in town." He opened the bottle, took a swig, and handed it to Tyler.

"Now you're talkin'," Tyler said. He took a long drink and then handed the bottle back to Erik. "So, what do you think? It's the apocalypse, the last stand, the proverbial end of fucking days... What do you miss most from the old world, besides friends, family, and normal human shit? We're being materialistic here, not philosophical."

Erik took a drink and thought about it. "I don't know... Music maybe? Those bagpipes we heard that night after the mansion got me thinking. I used to have a couple hundred songs downloaded on my phone. The good stuff they only play on the oldie's stations anymore. Pissed me off when they didn't let me bring it up to that camp with me. Now, even if I get home and find it again, it's not going to work." He handed the bottle back to Tyler. "You?"

"Video games," Tyler said without hesitation. "But maybe that's not so bad. Swear to God, I used to veg out for hours playing those damn things. It was a bad habit, more of an addiction, but I still miss it. I can't even guess how much money I spent on games over the years."

"And just think – all that money you spent on video games – imagine what you could do with it now."

"Oh wait," Tyler said, "let me think. I could buy... jack shit."

"And a lot of it."

They were both still laughing when Tyler suddenly stopped and said, "Listen."

Erik listened. From somewhere far to the east came a long, mournful howl.

"Coyote?" he asked.

"Wolf," Tyler said. "Man, those things are so cool. Nobody fucks with a wolf. I remember when I was like six or seven years old and my folks took me to a zoo. When we came to the wolves, I stood there watching them for the longest time. My dad had to drag me away. I begged them for months to get me a wolf for a pet." He laughed. "I wanted the most badass animal in the woods for a pet, and what did they get me? A beagle."

"Could have been worse. They could have gotten you a toy poodle."

"Or a chihuahua," Tyler agreed. "Man, I hate those barky little bastards. I think if I had to be reincarnated as any animal, it would be a wolf."

"What about a bear? I would think a grizzly bear could kick the shit out of a wolf."

"Only if it could catch it. But wolves are smarter. They hunt in packs. Ain't no grizzly going to fuck with a pack of wolves."

"Okay," Erik said. "You come back as a wolf and I'll be a bear. We'll have a smack-down and see who comes out on top."

"You're on!"

They continued passing the bottle of brandy back and forth. As full darkness filled the woods, the fire burned down and the bottle neared empty. After about an hour, the conversation took its inevitable turn to girls.

"Remember that girl I told you about," Tyler said, "the one that belted me at the basketball game when I kissed her?"

"Hey, seeing as where we are now, I'd say it was worth a shot."

"Yeah, it was." He paused and then continued. "Her name was Jackie. I don't know. I've always had this feeling that if I hadn't blown it then, if I'd just bided my time and waited, things might have been different."

"Maybe," Erik said, "maybe not. Hell, if her friends hadn't been with her that night, you two might have ended up making out right there on the bleachers. Or under the bleachers."

"You think so?"

"No, not really. I think she still would have gotten pissed. Maybe she wouldn't have belted you one but… well, you took a shot and you missed. You get what you get when you go for it."

Tyler stared at him over the dwindling fire, furrowing his brows.

"Did you just fucking quote Barry Manilow at me?"

Erik laughed. "Hey, Barry's got a song for every occasion."

"Bullshit. How about the apocalypse?"

"*Looks Like We Made It.*"

"When that psycho cult attacked us."

"*Do You Know Who's Livin' Next Door?*"

"When you and Ashley had sex."

Erik almost replied with *Somewhere in the Night*, but then caught himself and grinned.

"Nice try, dick-weed."

"You're still not denying it."

The snap of a twig from the trees behind Tyler caused him to whirl around. A heavily bearded man roughly the size of a bear, wearing camouflage bib overalls and a grimy Cat baseball cap, stepped out of the darkness. He said nothing but held a shotgun at his side, leveled at Tyler.

Erik jumped to his feet and reached for his pistol. He froze as he felt the cold steel of a gun barrel press against the back of his neck.

"You just take it easy there, boy," a voice behind him growled. "You twitch so much as a finger and I'll blow your goddamn head off."

Erik heard the double click of a rifle hammer being cocked back.

***

Erik slowly moved his hand away from his pistol.

The man behind him stepped around to his side, keeping his rifle pointed at Erik's head. He was a small, wiry man with long, ratty, light brown hair and a scraggly beard. He looked like he hadn't bathed since even a month or two before the storm.

"You keep that one covered, Del," the man said, keeping his eyes on Erik. "If he moves, you make sure he never moves again." He jabbed his rifle toward Erik. "You. Reach down there real slow and take that pistol out of your belt with two fingers. Throw it on the ground there in front of you."

Erik did as he was told. He remembered that Red had said there were three men, a tall one, a short one, and a fat one. If these were the same men, he wondered where the tall one was.

"Step back," the man said, motioning with his rifle. When Erik did, the man stepped forward and snatched his pistol up from the ground. He stuffed the barrel into the front of his pants and then stepped back, raising his rifle to Erik again. "Del," he called back to the other man, "you get that one's pistol."

The fat man, Del, prodded Tyler with his shotgun.

Tyler took his own pistol from its holster and held it out to Del. As Del reached for it, Tyler dropped it to the ground.

Del growled in his throat and pushed the barrels of his shotgun into Tyler's chest, shoving him back. He then picked the pistol up and stuffed it into a pocket of his coveralls.

The short man relaxed a bit. He lowered his rifle to his side but kept it pointed in Erik's direction.

"Okay. Now you boys are gonna get your packs on and you're gonna come with us up the road there into town. You try to run or do anything stupid and Del there is gonna take you out at the knees. Understand?"

Erik nodded.

The man looked to Tyler. "Understand?" he repeated with a little more emphasis.

Tyler snorted but then gave a single, short nod.

The man motioned with his rifle for the boys to get their backpacks on. As they did, he stepped quickly back into the darkened tree line and re-emerged holding a lantern with a red, glass chimney.

"You two follow me. Del will be right behind you with that shotgun. You remember that if you start to get any ideas."

Erik and Tyler followed the short man back up to the road while Del followed behind with his shotgun. Seeing the light cast by the lantern, Erik understood how the men had been able to navigate the darkness without being seen. The reddish light allowed them to see about five or six feet ahead but couldn't be seen from more than a few yards away. It was perfect for sneaking up on two idiot boys laughing and drinking brandy around a campfire.

The men led them up the road and into town, coming to a large, two-story home with an open front deck that spanned the width of the house. Light was coming from most of the windows on the first floor. Rather than hiding their presence as Erik and Tyler had been doing, these guys were practically advertising it.

The smaller man banged on the door with the butt of his rifle. "It's Lou," he hollered.

After a minute or two the door opened and a tall, broad-shouldered man stepped into the doorway, silhouetted in the darkness. Erik guessed he had to be close to seven feet tall. Because of the backlight, he couldn't see any other features.

"We found 'em, Abe," the short man, Lou, said. "They were down by the creek, just like you said."

The tall man, Abe, sized them up with a long, steady look.

"Were they armed?" he asked in an oddly casual baritone voice.

"Couple of pistols is all," Lou said, indicating Erik's .44 in his belt.

Abe nodded. "Bring them in." He turned and disappeared back into the house.

Del motioned with his shotgun and the boys followed Lou to a spacious room lined with bookshelves. There were two black leather couches and three padded chairs sitting around a large square table made of dark wood.

On the couches and chairs sat half a dozen mummified corpses. There was one man, three women, and two young girls. The man was wearing a suit and tie while the women were wearing blue, green, and red dresses. The two girls wore matching white dresses, white stockings, and black shoes they might have once worn to Sunday school.

Thoughts of Crazy Bob's dinner party in the park went through Erik's mind. He wondered if these corpses were all from this house or if they had been brought in from other houses.

Across the room, Abe was standing next to a large, granite fireplace that held a roaring log fire. He was pouring himself a drink from a glass decanter. From its brownish color, Erik guessed it was either bourbon or scotch. It idly occurred to him that he'd become somewhat of an expert in alcohol these past few weeks.

Lou led them to the table in the center of the room and indicated where they should stand. Del stood behind them and off to the side. His shotgun was still leveled on them.

Abe turned to look into the fireplace, swirling the drink in his glass. "See what they're carrying," he said without turning around.

"Drop your packs," Lou ordered.

After they placed their backpacks on the floor, Lou upended them and dumped their contents onto the table. He took the two halves of the rifle and stared at them before tossing them back onto the pile. Erik guessed he probably thought it was broken, too dimwitted to know it was designed to come apart like that.

Lou pawed through their supplies and picked out the two bottles of mead Red had given them and the bottle of rye whiskey from the mansion.

"Well now," He said. "You boys know you're too young to be drinking this stuff." He took the bottles and placed them on the table next to Abe. "Just a broken rifle, food, clothes, and other stuff," he said. "And these."

Abe took the bottle of whiskey and studied the label, then set it back down on the table. As he did, he turned a little and Erik finally got a good look at his face. He had jet-black hair, a short beard, and an angular nose. He had a square jaw and a face that was creased and weathered, almost leathery, with irregular patches of brown on it. His eyes were almost completely white with small, faded black pupils in the centers.

It was the same as Erik had seen on the crazy woman in Milaca and Doctor Barrett back at the mansion. He guessed Abe had been affected by the storm and wondered how the man was still alive. He also wondered if "Abe" wasn't just a nickname, given his striking though somewhat deranged resemblance to a dead president.

Abe turned back to the fire and continued staring into it for a while. Erik noted how Lou and Del waited patiently for him to speak again, as if Abe was some sort of messianic figure and they were his apostles. His thoughts went back to Sister Angie's cult of women and their bodyguards. The end of the world certainly seemed to bring out the psychotic nut-jobs.

Abe turned and began to make a slow circuit of the room, glass in hand and head down as if in deep thought. He paused before each corpse and stared at it for a few seconds before moving on to the next. Somewhere around the fourth or fifth corpse, Erik got the impression that Abe was, or at least thought he was, communicating with each, perhaps telepathically.

Jesus, he thought. *This one's gone all the way down the rabbit hole.*

He glanced at Tyler and could tell that he'd come to the same conclusion.

When Abe reached the corpse of the man, he stopped and "communicated" with him a little longer than the rest before returning to his original place in front of the fire. When he spoke again, he was looking down at the floor, somewhat in the direction of Lou's feet.

"Why are they here?" he asked in that low, casual voice.

Lou turned to Erik and Tyler.

"Why are you here?"

Tyler glanced at Erik and grinned. "Seriously?" He looked at Lou. "We're here because you and your boyfriend, large Marge over there, dragged us here at gunpoint. What are you, fucking stupid?"

Lou's face flushed red and he glanced to Abe. Without looking up, Abe gave a slight nod.

Lou backhanded Tyler across the face. Tyler stumbled back into Del, who shoved him forward again with his shotgun.

"I'm going to ask you again, smart ass," Lou said, getting in Tyler's face. "What are you doing here?"

Tyler glared at Lou. Erik could see he was on the verge of knocking some of Lou's crooked, brown teeth out of his mouth, which would only end in a couple of shotgun blasts and a lot of blood.

"We're heading south," Erik said quickly.

Lou turned slowly to Erik, staring at him with wide eyes as though Erik was some strange, ugly bug. He took a step back and pulled Erik's pistol from his waistband. He pointed it at Erik's head.

"Was I talking to you, dipshit?"

He thumbed the hammer back and Erik saw the cylinder rotate. The hollow-point bullets he'd loaded into each chamber yesterday looked as large as cannon balls.

"We're heading to Iowa," Tyler said, "following the highway."

Lou turned his gaze back to Tyler, keeping the pistol pointed at Erik. He glared at him before glancing back to Abe.

Abe turned and walked over to the couch, stopping in front of the corpses of the two young girls.

Lou scowled at Erik and made a show of uncocking the pistol in front of his face before lowering it.

Abe stared down at the girls, seemingly lost in thought, before leaning down to the one on his right and placing his forehead against hers. He closed his eyes for several seconds before opening them again and raising his head slightly. He placed his fingers under the girl's chin, leaned forward, and kissed her lightly on her tight, leathery lips.

"Thank you," he whispered to the corpse.

He straightened and signaled to Lou with a slight sideways nod of his head.

Lou looked at Erik and Tyler and grinned. "Let's go, boys." He waved the pistol toward the doorway.

They followed Lou out of the room, with Del and his shotgun bringing up the rear again.

Tyler tipped his head toward Erik as they walked and whispered, "I don't know about you, but that guy is one creepy-ass motherfucker."

Erik nodded in agreement. He was trying to think of a way out of this mess. He figured either he or Tyler could easily overpower the smaller man, but Del outweighed both of them together by at least a hundred pounds. Even if they could get their hands on his shotgun, it was a good bet he would still be able to kill at least one of them with his bare hands before they could take him down.

Lou led them down a hallway toward the back of the house. He stopped in front of a closed door and rapped on it with his knuckles.

"Annabelle?" he called, showing his dirty, crooked-tooth grin. "Are you decent? We've got some roommates for you." He took a key from his pocket and unlocked the door. As he pushed it open, the smell of decomposition filled the hallway.

He stepped aside and Del used his shotgun to push the boys into the room. The stench was suffocating. Before Erik could see what was in the room with them, Lou pulled the door closed, cutting off the light. Erik heard the key turn in the lock.

Lou's voice called from the other side of the door. "Now you boys make yourselves comfortable in there and don't you be teasing Annabelle. She's real sensitive about her looks."

His cackling laughter trailed off as he and Del went back up the hallway.

***

Tyler's voice came from the darkness. "Jesus, what is that smell?"

Erik dug for the lighter in his pocket, found it, and flicked it on.

They were in a small, windowless room. Probably an old storage room, Erik thought, judging by the empty shelves along three of the walls. He saw Tyler. The left side of his face was red and a little swollen from where Lou had backhanded him.

Erik turned and held the lighter out. The flickering light fell on the corpse of a woman propped up in the corner. She wasn't a mummy but she was certainly dead. She looked like she had been in her mid-twenties and had short brown hair. She was wearing a dirty white dress that was too small for her, a black belt around her waist, white socks, and black shoes – dressed exactly like the two girls in Abe's little menagerie in the other room.

"God," Erik said. "She's been dead a while. A week, at least."

"Must be Annabelle," Tyler said, "if that really was her name. I get the feeling these guys aren't much for getting to know their victims."

"Hey, man," Erik said. "First chance we get, we've got to try and get out of here."

"Are you serious? Like you think you need to tell me that?"

"I mean, even if it comes to taking a gut-full of buckshot from large Marge, we've got to do something. I'd rather die trying to take one of them down with me than end up like Annabelle here, or that family we came across."

"You want to try and rush them when they come back for us?"

"We'll play it by ear," Erik said. "Whoever sees an opportunity, take it. Whatever I do, you back me up. Whatever you do, I'll back you up."

"First one to kill that little weasel that hit me gets a cold beer."

They sat down on opposite sides of the room, on either side of the door. It was Tyler's idea, figuring the more space there was between them, the better their odds of at least one of them being able to tackle whoever opened the door.

Erik clicked the lighter off and they sat in the darkness in silence. He had thought he would get used to the smell after a while but it wasn't happening.

He played out different scenarios in his head, of either one or the other or both of the men coming into the room and he and Tyler attacking them. The only scenario he could see where they both escaped was if the weasel, Lou, was dumb enough to come into the room alone and the big man, Del, was nowhere in sight. Even then, either he or Tyler was likely to take a bullet. And then there was the problem of getting past Del and Abe without knowing exactly where they were in the house.

After what felt like two or three hours but was probably much less, Erik felt himself starting to doze off despite the smell of the rotting corpse next to him. He had to stay awake, alert.

"Tyler," he said. "Are you awake?"

Tyler's voice came out of the darkness. "Yeah."

"I'm sorry, man. It was my idea where we camped and I'm the one who decided we should drink that brandy. If we'd been a little more alert... I guess I am Frodo after all."

Tyler chuckled in the darkness. "Yeah, you are. But as Samwise, I should be saving your ass right about now. I'm not seeing that happening."

A thump against the door cut them off and Erik quickly got to his feet. He heard Tyler do the same across the room.

The lock clicked and the door swung open. The light from Lou's lantern briefly blinded Erik but he could still see the hulking shape of Del right behind the smaller man, his shotgun resting in the crook of his arm.

Lou, holding the lantern in one hand and Erik's forty-four-magnum in the other, leaned heavily against the doorway and waved the gun at Tyler.

"You, smart mouth. Let's go."

He looked unsteady on his feet and Erik guessed he was drunk. And the way Dell was holding his shotgun, not ready at all… This was probably their best and only chance.

As Tyler stepped toward the door, Erik took a careful step to the side, ready to charge the men in the narrow hallway. He figured he could easily knock Lou to the floor and then Tyler could grab his gun. Erik would attack Dell and tie him up long enough for Tyler to blow him away.

Tyler saw his movement and gave a quick shake of his head.

Erik stopped and stayed where he was. Did Tyler have a different plan?

Lou grinned and rolled his head, watching as Tyler stepped past him. He then glanced back into the room at Erik.

"Keep your panties on, petunia. Your turn will come soon enough." He barked a quick laugh and then closed the door and locked it.

Shit, Erik thought. *Shit-shit-shit.* He should have charged the door anyway. What in hell was Tyler thinking? They were drunk. He and Tyler could have easily overpowered the two. Instead, Tyler had let them take him without so much as one of his usual snide comments.

Damn it! Erik paced the room in the darkness. He wanted to scream, to hit something. When they came back for him, he was going to rush the door no matter what Tyler wanted. There was no way he was going to go down without a fight.

He continued pacing, waiting, listening for the key turning in the lock. He was amped up and ready to jump, psyching himself up for what he knew would be a life or death confrontation.

After about ten minutes, the muffled sound of a gunshot from somewhere in the house brought his pacing to a sudden halt. He froze and put every ounce of energy into listening. There was a second shot, followed closely by two more. They were deep, booming sounds that reverberated in the walls and the floor – the sound of either a forty-four-magnum or a shotgun, or both.

A minute or two later, a fifth shot came from another part of the house. Erik cocked his head, listening. Was Tyler running? Was he running from room to room while Lou shot at him with Erik's pistol? Or was Del blasting away with the shotgun?

Almost a minute passed and then Erik heard a sixth shot. What in the hell was going on out there? God, he wanted to scream, to bash this door down, to do *something*.

Five minutes passed, then ten. Erik started pacing again. After what felt like an hour, he heard the key turning in the lock. He steeled himself for what would almost certainly be a suicide charge. He would use his hands, his feet, his teeth... whatever it took.

The door swung open and Tyler was standing there, silhouetted against the light from the lantern on the floor behind him, leaning casually against the wall. He had a lopsided grin on his face and Erik's forty-four magnum in his hand.

"They did *not* know who they were fucking with," Tyler said.

***

"Are you waiting for a pizza or something?" Tyler motioned with the gun. "As you like to say, let's get the fuck out of here."

Erik stepped to the doorway. "What happened?" he asked, still shocked at seeing Tyler alive.

Tyler grinned and reached under his jacket. He pulled the Bowie knife from its sheath on his belt. It was smeared with blood.

"Figured that little bastard for a rapist. Probably should have searched me before telling his buddy to wait outside and dropping his pants."

"Jesus. Did you get them all?"

Tyler nodded. "Gutted that little fucker like a trout, then took his gun – your gun, this gun – and put one between his eyes to make sure. Figured that would bring that big bastard through the door. Took two shots to drop him."

"What about Abe?"

"Crazy son of a bitch was still standing in the library, drinking our whiskey. Didn't even turn or anything. He kept staring into the fire." Tyler shook his head. "He had to have heard the shots. He had to have known I was behind him, but he just stood there like some fucked-up stoner or something. I shot him in the back and he collapsed like a sack of potatoes. Must have severed his spine 'cause he was still alive when I walked up to check him. Fucker still wouldn't look at me even when I stood over him. He kept staring at the corpses of those two girls, reaching out to them like they could save his ass or something. Crazy goddamned bastard. I put one between *his* eyes too."

He tossed Erik's pistol to him. "Saved your life. Debt re-paid."

Erik caught the pistol. "Never said you owed me anything, dipshit." He pushed the pistol into the waistband of his jeans. He was going to have to reload it after he retrieved his backpack.

"You knew that little shit was going to try and rape you and you planned this, didn't you?"

Tyler shrugged. "Sorry. Figured there was a better chance of him choosing me over you, seeing as I'm the one who pissed him off earlier. If I'd told you, you would have tried to be the hero and do it yourself." A fit of coughing hit him and he leaned forward, grimacing in pain and holding his side. When he looked back up, there was blood on his mouth and chin.

A jolt of fear went through Erik. "Christ, are you shot?" He looked and saw the side of Tyler's shirt and pants were soaked in blood.

Tyler coughed again, spraying blood but managing a grin. "Yeah, that big fucker caught me with his shotgun. Think he only grazed me though. It's not too bad." But even as he spoke, his knees started to buckle.

Erik caught him and threw Tyler's arm across his shoulder.

"Come on. Let's get you into the light and get that cleaned up." He grabbed the lantern and helped Tyler down the hallway.

In the kitchen, he set Tyler in a chair at a small, round table and began running water in the sink without even considering if this town had running water or not.

He pulled Tyler's jacket and shirt off and then examined the wound. It was more than just a graze and a long way from "not too bad." Tyler had taken almost a full load of buckshot just below his ribs. His left side looked like raw hamburger.

"Damn, man." He tried not to sound as scared as he felt. He soaked a kitchen towel in the sink and started cleaning the wound. "This is bad."

Tyler laughed and then coughed. "Don't try to sugar-coat it, doc. Give it to me straight."

"You need to lay down. I'll try to stop the bleeding but, shit, I don't know. I wish Saundra was here."

Erik wrapped towels around Tyler's abdomen as tight as he could and then ran back to where Lou had dumped their backpacks, glancing only briefly at the mute corpses and the body of Abe lying on the floor. He grabbed one of the first aid kits and returned to the kitchen.

Inside the kit was a tube of anti-bacterial gel, some antiseptic wipes, gauze, bandages, and other supplies. Erik removed the wet towels from Tyler's side and used the antiseptic wipes to clean the wound better. He then spread the anti-bacterial gel on some gauze and dressed the wound as best he could but blood continued to ooze out around the sides of the bandages.

He eased Tyler to his feet and helped him to the master bedroom – probably where Abe had been sleeping – and got him up onto the bed and covered with blankets. He went back to the kitchen and found a bottle of acetaminophen in the kit. Bringing the bottle and a glass of water back to the bedroom, he helped Tyler take four of the pills.

"What the hell are these?" Tyler asked, squinting at one. "Aspirin?"

"Acetaminophen," Erik said. "Aspirin's a blood thinner and that's the last thing you need right now."

"How the fuck do you know these things?"

"My mom's a nurse, remember? I've picked up a few tidbits over the years."

"I'll be fine," Tyler said, closing his eyes and sounding spent. He looked like he was about to fall asleep. "I don't think he hit anything vital. Besides, I've died before and it didn't feel anything like this."

"What?" Erik wondered if he was getting delirious. "What in hell are you talking about?"

Tyler grinned and opened his eyes about halfway.

"Didn't know you were partners with a zombie, did you?" He laughed and winced at the pain. "Couple years ago... fucking had a heart attack. Can you believe that? I'm fucking fourteen years old, playing basketball with a couple of guys in a driveway, and I have a goddamn heart attack while I'm charging in for a layup."

He gave a snorting laugh and winced again. "They said I was dead for almost ten minutes before they shocked me back to life. See that?" He pushed the covers down and pointed to a long, thick scar down the center of his chest. "Had some kind of narrow vein or something. They said I probably had it since I was born. Heart wasn't getting enough blood. They fixed it and now here I am, saving your ass from a weasel rapist, a mute fat man, and a psycho dead president."

"You saved both of our asses," Erik said, pulling the covers back over him. "Pat yourself on the back later. You need to sleep now."

"Don't let no one tell you there's no life after death," Tyler said, closing his eyes. "I've seen it. Have to tell you about it sometime. Pretty fucking cool." He looked like he was about to say something more but then drifted off to sleep.

Erik stayed with him for a while, watching to make sure his breathing remained steady. He checked Tyler's pulse. It felt steady and strong. After an hour or so, he left and began making his way from room to room.

Del lay inside the doorway of a bedroom at the other end of the house, just as Tyler said. He had been shot twice in the chest. His shotgun lay by his side.

Lou was lying on his back next to the bed in a massive pool of blood. His pants were down around his knees. He had been stabbed five or six times and sliced open from groin to sternum. Between his eyes was a neat, round hole about the size of a nickel. His brains and the back of his skull were splashed across the floor.

Erik went back to the library where they'd first been taken. The fire in the fireplace was still burning but growing smaller. The corpses – Abe's menagerie – sat in their couches and chairs, staring mutely at the dying fire. Lying on the floor in front of the fireplace was Abe, his legs bent awkwardly under him, one arm outstretched toward the two little-girl corpses. Erik felt a slight chill go down his spine. Abe was lying in almost the exact same position as Emily back in the little store along the highway. What were the odds of that?

Abe had a large hole in his gut where Tyler's first shot to his spine had exited and a neat, round hole in his forehead where the kill-shot had been administered. Pieces of his intestines, chunks of red flesh, gray brain matter, and white splinters of bone were splattered all around the body. Spilled whiskey and a broken glass lay nearby.

Both bottles of mead were missing from the table. That must have been what Del and Lou had been drunk on. Erik silently thanked Red for his generosity and Red's brother for making it as strong as he did.

He took the open bottle of rye whiskey from the table and returned to the master bedroom. Taking a sip from the bottle every now and then, he sat vigil over Tyler, watching his breathing and checking his pulse every five or ten minutes.

The thought of losing his friend kept him awake through the entire night.

JULY 21

The body hit the pavement with a sickening thud and the crack of bones breaking.

Erik clamped Tyler's Bowie knife between his teeth and carefully shinnied back down the light pole. Thank God that was the last of them. He hated having to let the bodies fall like that but there was no other way of getting them down.

Back on the street, he stuck the knife into his belt and took a couple of minutes to rest. The body he'd just cut down was a teenage boy, maybe a year or two older than himself. He looked like he'd been dead for at least a week. Erik wondered if he'd lived in this town – maybe he'd known Annabelle – or if Abe and company had taken him prisoner somewhere else and then brought him here. Either way, he couldn't imagine the terror the boy had probably gone through before they'd finally killed him.

He took the rope the boy had been hanging by, wrapped it around himself twice, and then threw the end over his own shoulder. He dragged the body up the street to the growing pile of corpses and kindling. It was undignified as all hell, like he was dragging a dead deer through the woods, but it was the best he could do by himself.

Several other bodies were already on the pile – two men, two women, three younger girls, and a little boy no older than Seth. None of them were mummies. They had all been hung from light poles up and down either side of the street. Annabelle from the storage room was among them. The mummified corpses from the library and the hanged carcasses of two dogs and a cat also lay on the pile. The murderous trio had spared no one.

He hefted the boy's body onto the pile and then stepped back to catch his breath and rest again. It was another cold day but he was sweating through his t-shirt. He'd been at this for a couple of hours now and his arms, shoulders, and legs were burning from the effort.

The morning after the shootout with the gruesome three, Tyler had developed a fever and became delirious. Erik found some rubbing alcohol and antibiotics in a medicine cabinet and had spent most of the next two days keeping Tyler's wound clean and disinfected while also trying to keep him drinking water and taking the antibiotics and pain killers. In between his nursing duties, he had dragged the bodies of Annabelle and her three murderers outside and onto the front lawn. It was the first time he'd been outside the house in the daytime and that's when he'd seen the corpses hanging from the light poles.

He'd left the bodies hanging until this morning when Tyler's fever seemed to be subsiding and he was sleeping more restfully. Using books from the home's library and breaking apart the bookshelves and some tables and chairs for wood, he'd built the funeral pyre on the street in front of the house. He'd brought out the corpses from the library and then used Tyler's knife and set about cutting the hanged bodies down. Erik guessed Abe and his buddies didn't hang them from the light poles as a warning to others. More likely, they did it because they were psychotic, murderous sons of bitches who probably thought it was funny.

Beginning to feel the chill again, Erik set about finishing what he'd started. He poured two five-gallon cans of diesel fuel he'd found in the garage onto the pile and touched his lighter to it. He watched the fire for a few minutes and then turned and headed back to the house.

He had left the bodies of Abe, Lou, and Dell on the front lawn next to the sidewalk. They didn't deserve any sort of funeral. Rather than cremate them on the pyre with their victims, Erik had decided their bodies would be more useful first as a common toilet and then as food for any scavengers that might come by later. Before going back into the house, he stopped and unzipped his pants. For the third time that day, he urinated on the bodies, making sure to give each of their faces a good hosing-down.

Tyler was sitting at the kitchen table, spreading peanut butter on crackers and wolfing them down between swigs from a gallon jug of orange juice.

"Holy shit, it lives!" Erik took a bottle of water from the counter and joined him at the table. "You know how long you were out?"

Tyler shook his head, unable to speak through a mouthful of crackers and peanut butter.

"You've been at death's door for three days, not counting this morning."

Tyler considered this and then shrugged. He washed the crackers down with a mouthful of orange juice and wiped his mouth with his arm.

"Did anyone call? Come to visit? Send cards or flowers?"

"Nope. I guess no one gives a shit about you."

"Fuck 'em, then. I don't need their pity." He stuffed another cracker into his mouth and eyed Erik. "What the hell have you been up to? You're sweatin' like a pig."

"Pigs don't sweat, you uneducated simpleton. And, if you must know, I've been taking care of your sorry ass while dragging Larry, Curly, and

Moe's stinking corpses out of the house. I've also been cutting their victims down from the light poles all up and down the street and burning the bodies. There's a bonfire out there right now. Did you know they had people hanging from the light poles out there? Dogs and cats too"

Tyler shook his head. "Somehow, that does not surprise me."

"Yeah, well, I also took that girl out of the storage room. I put her, Abe's corpse-family, and all the other bodies I could find on a big funeral pyre right out there in the street. Figured it's the least we could do, rather than leave them for the flies, assuming there are any flies still around."

"What about psycho Abe and the crazy twins?"

"They're out on the lawn, right by the sidewalk. And by the way, if you have to take a piss, the new toilet is out on the lawn, right by the sidewalk. I've been using it all day."

Tyler upended the box of crackers and shook it. He'd eaten them all. He glanced around the kitchen for more food and stood up, wincing a little from the pain at his side.

"I don't think you should be moving around too much," Erik said. "I don't know anything about stitching, so those bandages are pretty much the only thing holding you together. Plus, I'm pretty sure all that buckshot is still rolling around inside you somewhere."

"It's not bleeding anymore," Tyler said, snagging a package of beef jerky from the counter and making his way back to the table. "Besides, I looked at it this morning and it looks like it's not much more than a bad flesh wound. I don't think it did any real damage inside."

"You didn't see it when it was fresh. Looked like five pounds of raw hamburger. You were coughing up blood and you had a pretty good fever there for a while, sweating like hell and thrashing all over the bed. I've had to shove pills and water down your throat the past couple of days."

"You lie. I don't remember that at all."

"You don't remember it because you were unconscious most of the time. Either way, you should probably take it easy for a while. But if you insist on getting up and moving around, move your ass down the hall and take a bath. You reek about as bad as those bodies out there on the lawn."

JULY 23

"I'm not a fucking invalid," Tyler complained. "I can carry my own shit."

"We'll see how it goes the first day," Erik said, taking the bottles of water from Tyler's backpack and stuffing them into his own. "If you're still on your feet by sunset, then maybe I'll let you carry the map."

"Can I at least carry my own gun?"

"Is it loaded?"

"Of course."

"Then no, hand it over."

"Fuck you. I may have to save your ass again." Tyler defiantly jammed the pistol into his holster. He picked up his backpack and frowned. It looked deflated, holding only a couple of clean t-shirts, a box of bandages, and the bottles of pain killers, antibiotics, and rubbing alcohol. "This is pathetic. A five-year-old girl could carry more than this."

"A five-year-old girl that didn't take a load of buckshot to the side," Erik said. "You're lucky that big bastard didn't take time to aim before pulling the trigger." He zipped his own backpack closed and hefted it to his shoulders. It was bulging with enough supplies for the both of them and at least twice as heavy as he was accustomed to carrying.

Erik couldn't carry both sleeping bags so he allowed Tyler to carry his own. He had misgivings about heading back out on the road this morning but Tyler was insistent he was fine – he was itching to get out of this house and this town. Erik had to admit he was starting to go a little stir-crazy himself.

Tyler had steadily improved over the last couple of days and could now walk and move about without much pain. Erik was still worried about his stamina and strength though. From his own experience with a major injury – shattering his hip in that fall from the tree – he knew bed rest could weaken a person. But since Tyler insisted on getting out of here and on the road again, there was little Erik could do but compromise and insist that he carry most of the weight himself. He'd also made sure Tyler understood they would be taking it slow and with frequent breaks.

When they left the house, they both took a couple of minutes to urinate one last time on the faces of Abe, Del, and Lou. As they did, Erik commented he was hoping scavengers like coyotes and crows would eventually come along and dispose of the bodies and scatter the bones.

"Won't happen," Tyler said, shaking his head. "Scavengers only eat dead things. They don't eat shit."

They followed the street back to the highway and continued south out of town. As they walked, Erik kept an eye on Tyler, calling for a break every time it looked like he was sweating too much or breathing too hard. By midday, when Erik called for a longer rest break and lunch, they had covered only about four miles.

"You know," Tyler said, "if you keep stopping us every fifteen minutes, the damn apocalypse will be over by the time we get you to Iowa. Your sister will be married and have kids of her own."

Erik reluctantly agreed to let Tyler call the breaks for the rest of the day. "But," he added, "if you look like you're about to keel over because you're trying to be all macho and shit, we're stopping for the rest of the day and pitching camp on the spot."

They started out again and Tyler kept a slow but steady pace for a couple of hours before stopping for a few minutes. He was sweating but he wasn't out of breath and did not look ready to pass out. His improved stamina impressed Erik, especially considering how out of shape Tyler had been when they'd first left Aitken. God, how long ago had that been? Five weeks? Six? More?

By late afternoon, they had covered nearly ten miles, leaving the corn fields behind, and were now passing through a stretch of woods. They stopped on a narrow concrete bridge that passed over another dry creek bed to take a brief rest before scouting a place to camp for the night. Erik checked his map and discovered they were only a couple miles west of I-35, which would lead them straight south into Iowa.

"Believe it or not, I think we're about halfway there," Erik said, re-folding the map and stowing it back into his pack.

"Hooray for our side. Mordor awaits." Tyler's voice sounded strained, weak.

Erik glanced at him and was shocked at how pale Tyler's face suddenly was. He was leaning back against the side of the bridge, his face and shirt drenched with sweat. His breathing seemed way too rapid and shallow.

"Man, you need to sit down right now," Erik said, alarmed. He hadn't been watching Tyler closely for the past hour or so, having assumed he was doing fine. But now, it was obvious he should have been watching because Tyler had pushed himself too far.

Tyler leaned forward, his hands on his knees, catching his breath. He raised one hand and waved it weakly at Erik. "I'll be okay… just need to… take a break." He straightened back up and appeared to be trying to take a deep breath when his eyes suddenly rolled back in his head and he toppled backwards off the bridge.

"Oh Jesus," Erik groaned, quickly shedding his backpack and running to the side.

He could hear Tyler crashing through the brush below and then the sound of rocks being scattered about. Leaning over the side of the bridge, he searched the trees and brush nearly forty feet below until locating Tyler lying in the rocky bed of the small creek near the bottom of a steep embankment.

"God *damn* it!"

He hurried to the end of the bridge and then ran, jumped, and stumbled all the way down the embankment to the creek bed.

Tyler was lying on his side, not moving. The way his right arm was bent, Erik was sure it was broken. He carefully rolled Tyler onto his back and saw the side of his shirt was soaked with blood underneath his jacket.

Tyler's eyes fluttered open. He looked confused. Then he focused on Erik's face.

"What?" he asked in a raspy voice. "Did I pass out?"

"You fell off the fucking bridge, you moron," Erik said. He was relieved that Tyler was awake and talking but scared at what he was seeing. Something in his gut was telling him this wasn't just serious, this was end-of-the-road serious. "You've got a broken arm and you're bleeding like a stuck pig. Jesus, you should have taken a break sooner. You pushed yourself too hard."

"Ah, shit. My dad always said I was too stubborn to know when to quit. Guess he was right." His eyes moved around, as if seeing how things looked from the flat of his back in a dry creek bed. "You know," he said, looking back to Erik, "now that you mention it, I think I am fucked. I can't feel my arms or legs."

Erik glanced back up the side of the embankment and saw Tyler's backpack. It had been ripped from his shoulders in his tumble down the side. "Hold on," he said. He retrieved the backpack and carefully positioned it under Tyler's head as a makeshift pillow. "Do you want some water? I'll have to go back up to the bridge and get my pack."

Tyler managed a lazy shake of his head. "Don't bother. I won't be around long enough. I can feel it."

"Feel what?"

"It's no big deal. I told you... I've died before." He was wracked by a short spasm of coughing and took a few labored breaths. Blood trickled from the corner of his mouth. "I know this dance." His voice was suddenly weaker, raspier. He was struggling to breathe. "This is the end of the road for me."

"No," Erik moaned. His chest felt tight. He knew what Tyler was saying and he knew it was the truth, but he hated it with all his heart. "Don't you remember? Samwise doesn't die. He and Frodo both make it to the end. Samwise gets married. He has kids and grows old."

"Not this time. Sorry, buddy. I guess I'm not going to be finishing this journey with you after all." He gave a weak smile. "Sucks too, 'cause I kind of wanted to meet this sister of yours. She must be something special for you to go through this much hell. Might have even brought a tear to my eye watching you two find each other again."

Erik glanced up at the bridge and closed his eyes. He clenched his teeth, trying to maintain his composure. His throat felt thick and he could feel tears trying to force their way out.

When he looked down again, he saw Tyler's eyes were closed. For a second, he was sure Tyler had died, but then his eyes fluttered open again and he gave Erik a tired smile.

"So...," he said, barely above a whisper. "Are you going to admit it?"

"Admit what?"

"You... and Ashley..." He coughed. "Come on man. It's confession time. I'm dying to know." He almost chuckled at his own pun but grimaced in pain instead.

Erik shook his head. "Man, you won't let that go, will you?" He paused, then sighed and nodded. "Yeah, that night before we left, she came into our room. I woke up and she was in bed with me."

"No shit?" Tyler managed a grin. "Right there with me sleeping in the next bed? Damn, I knew you were a hound dog but Jesus..." He grimaced at the pain again, squeezing his eyes shut. When he opened them, he was looking past Erik, staring up to the sky.

"Fucking A...," he breathed.

"What?"

"Stars."

"What are you talking about?"

"Look up, goofus," he said in a bare whisper.

Erik looked up and was surprised it was already getting dark. But even more surprising, for the first time since the storm, there was a break in the constant haze. A small, clear patch had opened in the gray shroud over the earth. And in that small patch of sky, he saw what Tyler had seen – three stars shining brightly against the deepening blue of the evening sky.

"Hol-ly shit," Erik breathed, feeling a smile spread across his face. "Look at that!"

As he stared at the stars, he couldn't help but feel as though some higher power was at last smiling down upon them.

He looked back down to Tyler.

His smile turned more into a grimace and he closed his eyes, feeling the tears as they ran down his face.

Though Tyler's own eyes were still open, he could no longer see the stars.

Erik lifted him by the shoulders, carefully pulling Tyler closer so that his head was resting on Erik's chest.

He wrapped his arms around his friend and held him, rocking slowly from side to side, no longer trying to hold his tears back or wipe them away.

He thought he would sit here for a while, all night maybe, just him and Tyler. Looking up at the stars.

JULY 24

Erik used rocks from the creek bed to cover Tyler. He walked up and down the creek all throughout the next morning, selecting mostly smooth, rounded stones about the size of a softball and bringing them back a few at a time until the cairn was complete. He finished it off by placing a large, flat stone on top and scratching on it with Tyler's Bowie knife.

Gute reise, mein freund.

He stood quietly next to the cairn for a while, his hand resting on the flat stone, feeling its cold surface, his fingers tracing the letters.

"We did have a good journey, didn't we?" he whispered. "I wish you could have been with me to the end."

He transferred the sheath for the knife to his own belt and slid the knife in. Placing Tyler's backpack at the base of the cairn, he turned and climbed back up the embankment to retrieve his own pack. From the bridge, he took a few minutes to stare down at the pile of rocks, feeling sadder and more alone than he had at any time since the storm.

"Take care, buddy," he said softly. He touched his fingers to the side of his head and gave a kind of salute. "I'll miss you."

He turned and started back down the road, glancing up at the sky. It was late morning, almost noon now. More openings in the haze had appeared during the night, slowly spreading and joining with other openings. There was still a lot of gray up there but more and more of the sky was showing through all the time.

He zipped his jacket up. He hoped with the haze disappearing, it might finally start to warm up. But something told him not to count on it.

Within an hour, he reached the interstate and turned south again, walking in the middle of the road. It was now a straight shot into Iowa.

Somewhere along the road over the next few days, without consciously thinking about it, he made the decision to avoid towns and any places people might be for the rest of his journey. He still stopped at houses to scavenge for supplies over the following weeks but only if he was sure there was no one living there. He traveled alone, slept alone, and ate alone, determined not to encounter another living person for the remainder of his journey.

It was just easier that way.

AUGUST 23

Erik stood on the street at the end of the driveway of the house he hadn't seen in over three months, his hands in his pockets but forgetting the cold. It was overcast this morning with dark clouds that threatened snow. It had been more than a week since the last of the grainy, gray haze had disappeared.

He'd spent last night camped under the overpass where highway 210 crossed over I-35. He had been only about seven miles from home but he wanted to get here in the daytime, not in the evening.

His mother's car was in the driveway. It was covered with leaves and a fine layer of dust. Two of its tires were flat. They had a two-car garage but it was always filled with junk and overflow from the house. He remembered how his mother was always going to clean it out and throw all that junk away so she could park her car in it again, but that chore always seemed to get put off to the next weekend and then the next.

There were two large maple trees in the front yard, leafless now and looking winter bare. Sam's pink and white bicycle with its handlebar basket leaned against one of the trees. Dry leaves covered the yard and Sam's bike. More leaves were spilling out of its basket.

The house itself looked silent, still, empty, like every other house on the street. The windows were dark, flat panes of glass reflecting the cold world outside. Erik remembered how he and Sam would come home from school and Sam's cat would be sitting on the sill inside the big bay window. Spritz would watch them as they approached, turning his head to follow them all the way up the short, cobblestone sidewalk that ran from the driveway to the front deck. Then he would leap off the sill and dash to greet them at the door.

He smiled at the memory. He knew Spritz only ran to greet Sam. Anytime Erik came up the sidewalk alone, Spritz stayed where he was and regarded him with bored, disinterested eyes, never jumping down or rushing to greet him.

Erik would have given anything to see Spritz at the window now, staring at him with those cool, aloof eyes. But Spritz wasn't there and he tried not to think about how sad that made him feel.

He knew he was stalling. He had come all this way, walking hundreds of miles over the last three months to be here now. He was home, but now he was afraid to take the final few steps. He was afraid to walk through that door. He knew what he would find and then that would be the end, and he would have to accept the truth.

He breathed deep, held it, and then blew it out. His breath turned to fog in the cold air. Before he could consider it any longer, he hunched his backpack up higher on his shoulders and stepped forward onto the driveway. He kept moving, watching the driveway beneath his feet and then the cobblestones of the sidewalk, the steps of the front deck, and then he was at the door.

He pulled the storm door open and placed his hand on the latch of the front door. He hadn't thought about it until now but sometimes his mother locked the front door. Sometimes she didn't. A long time ago, he had carried a key to the door in his pocket but he had lost it somewhere along the way. Maybe it had been in the pocket of the jeans Saundra had ordered burned at the mansion.

Taking another slow breath, he squeezed the latch and pushed. The door swung open.

Erik stepped into the house, the entryway. It was gloomy inside. The air was still. The house was quiet. There were his mother's shoes on the floor. There were Sam's shoes and a pair of his own sneakers. There was Spritz's litter box next to the grandfather clock that had stopped at 2:17 in the morning over three months ago. Sam's raincoat and one of his own jackets and a baseball cap hung on the rack on the wall.

It was all so familiar, as though he had left for camp only a couple of days ago. He could see Sam running around the corner now. He would kneel and she would jump into his arms and he would hug her, telling her how much he had missed her. Sam would be asking him a million questions and Erik would look up to see his mother standing there, smiling, waiting for her chance to hug him and welcome him home.

He stood there, listening to the silence for a while. Then he slid his backpack off and placed it against the railing that ran along the stairwell to the basement. He turned and walked slowly through the living room, looking at everything, running his hand along the back of the couch. In the dining room, there were envelopes and papers on the table, along with a calculator, a pen, and his mother's checkbook. She always opened the mail and paid bills at the dining room table.

In the kitchen, there were clean dishes in the drainer by the sink and a few on the counter waiting to be washed. On the other counter next to the stove, where he and Sam would sit on stools and eat breakfast in the morning, there was an envelope propped up against the saltshaker. His name was written across the front in black marker. It was his father's handwriting.

Erik picked up the envelope and stared at it for a while before opening it and taking out the single sheet of paper it contained. It was a letter from his father. He sat down on one of the stools and read it.

> Erik,
> I don't know if you will ever read this but, if you do, it means you somehow survived and found your way back home. I can't imagine how you did it or what you must have gone through but, believe me, it does not surprise me. I've always known that you're smart and you have good instincts. You've never given up on anything and I know you won't give up now.
> I'm sorry to say your mother and sister did not survive whatever this was. I buried them in the garden out back. Maybe it's best they were taken quickly and they won't have to try to survive in this dead world now. Maybe they are blessed and we are cursed. I don't know.
> It's getting cold now and I think it will keep getting colder so I'm heading south, maybe to Kansas City. I'll follow I-35 as much as I can and watch for you. I hope you will follow. I would like to see you again.
> Whatever you decide, wherever you go, please know that I've always loved you. I'm proud of you. Don't ever give up.
> Love, Dad

Erik read the letter a second time, then folded it and put it back into the envelope. He sat for a while, not thinking anything. Then he laid the envelope on the counter and went out the kitchen door to the back deck. From there he could see across the backyard to his mother's garden. There were three mounds of dirt in it.

He went to the garden and stood between the graves of Sam and his mother. Each had been marked with a framed photo. The small grave next to Sam's was marked with a cat toy – a small, cloth mouse that could be filled with catnip.

Erik lowered himself to his knees and took Sam's picture from her grave, holding it carefully in his hands. It was a school portrait from last year. Her long blonde hair had been set in a slight curl for the picture. He remembered the day it was taken. She wore a pink dress with matching stockings and black shoes. It had rained the night before and she was afraid she would get her clothes dirty before pictures, so Erik had carried her from the house to the bus and then from the bus to the school. He smiled at the memory.

"I'm here, Sam," he whispered. "I'm home."

AUGUST 25

Erik walked through the house, taking one last look into every room. He had spent the last two days in a kind of melancholy funk, wandering around, touching things, remembering. He had slept in Sam's bed, crying himself to sleep each night. Now he understood how Tyler had so easily left his own home. There was nothing but memories here now, ghosts of a time he could never get back.

In his mother's room, he went through her jewelry box and found the silver chain and crucifix his father had helped him buy for a birthday present when he was seven years old. He unclasped the chain and slid the crucifix off, putting the little silver cross back into the jewelry box.

As he turned to leave the room, he caught a glimpse of himself in his mother's vanity mirror. He stopped, turned, and regarded the reflection. He looked almost ten years older now. He had lost weight. Months on the road had leaned him out, hardened him. His hair was long and slightly ratty. His face was narrower, sharper. And there was something about his eyes he no longer recognized. They looked like the eyes of someone much older, someone who had seen too much and who no longer gave a damn.

He went to Sam's room and looked through the drawers of her child-sized vanity. In with her plastic rings, hair ties, colorful bracelets, and necklaces, he found her magic bunny. That's what she called it and it was her most prized possession. It was an amethyst rabbit, only an inch long, deep violet in color and polished smooth. She'd found it at a garage sale last year and he'd bought it for her.

He removed the trinket from its silver-colored, plastic chain and held it in his hand, feeling its weight and smoothness between his fingers. He slid it onto his mother's silver chain and placed the chain around his neck.

In the kitchen, he took his backpack from the counter and shrugged it over his shoulders. When he'd arrived, it had been nearly empty. Now it was restocked with food, some water, Saundra's first aid kit, and a few other supplies he'd learned were helpful on the road. He slid the freshly sharpened Bowie knife back into its sheath and then picked up his forty-four magnum from the counter. He habitually checked that it was loaded and slid it into his holster.

He glanced around one last time, knowing he would never see this place again. Picking up Sam's copy of *Alice's Adventures in Wonderland,* he went out the kitchen door and crossed the backyard to the garden one last time.

As he had done the previous two nights, Erik knelt by Sam's grave and opened the book to where he'd left off. He read the last two chapters aloud, making sure to do the character voices the way she liked. When he was finished, he closed the book and laid it on her grave.

He turned to his mother's grave and picked up her picture.

"I love you, Mom. I'm sorry I never said that every day. Don't be sad about the things I've done. You did your best and that must have been good enough because I'm still here. Wherever you are now, please take care of Sam until I get there." He kissed the picture and placed it back on the grave.

He turned back to Sam's grave and picked up her picture. He held it for a while, touching her face with his finger. He knew he was crying again but he didn't care.

"Goodbye, Sam. You're my best friend and I wish I could have been here for you at the end. You will always be the best part of me."

He looked up at the sky. It was another cold day. It felt more like late November or early December than late August. There were deep blue-gray clouds in the sky but the sun was still shining through in places.

He looked down at Sam's picture again.

"I love you, Sam, and I'll miss you for the rest of my life. I have to go now but I'll find you someday. You mind Mom until I get there, okay? And don't feed Spritz too much. You know he's too fat already." He kissed her picture and set it back on the grave next to the book.

He stood and gazed down on the graves for a while longer. Then he turned and crossed the yard to the street. He headed east and then north towards the town of Slater. He wasn't sure exactly where he was going. He just knew that it was time to leave. He'd briefly thought about heading south, the direction his father had taken, but he felt something pulling him north, maybe back to Minnesota, maybe to South Dakota or Wisconsin. He didn't know where he would end up, but the most important lesson he'd learned these past few months was to always follow his gut.

A small herd of deer crossed the road ahead of him, moving from one dead cornfield to the next. They stopped briefly on the road and watched him cautiously but they didn't run. He saw there were two fawns with them. They must have been born in the past month or two. Only three months after the storm and life was already struggling back.

As he passed the local elementary school in Slater, he heard a cat yowling from back among the houses to his left. He continued walking for a ways, uninterested in what a cat would possibly be crying about, but then he heard it again and he stopped and listened more carefully. Now it sounded more like the crying of a child. Then he heard a woman's scream and the gruff, angry voice of a man.

He followed the sounds of crying across the yards and around to the back of an older two-story house. As he came around the corner, the first thing he saw was a woman lying face-down on the brown grass, either unconscious or dead. A few yards away, a large man was looming over a young girl. She was sitting on the ground, sobbing, trying to kick herself away from the man. He had her by one arm and was dragging her away from the woman.

Erik drew the .44 from his belt and strode forward, cocking and raising the pistol at the same time.

"Hey!" he shouted.

The man jerked around. His fat face was flushed red and his long, stringy hair hung down over his eyes. His look of surprise flashed to anger.

"Boy, you'd better…"

Whatever threat he'd been about to make was cut short by the booming sound of the magnum. The top half of his head disintegrated in a spray of red, white, and gray. A large chunk of his skull, stringy hair still attached, pinwheeled through the air and landed in some bushes. The rest of his bulky body collapsed in a heap next to the girl, almost landing on top of her. She scrambled backwards, away from the body.

Erik quickly re-holstered his pistol. Rather than approach the girl, he knelt at the side of the woman and examined her. Her skin was still warm to the touch but she was dead. It looked like she'd taken a massive blow to the side of the head by some heavy object or, more likely, the fat man's fist. A cloth tote bag lay on the ground next to her, cans of pasta, corn, and chili spilling from it.

Staying crouched, he turned to the girl. She was sitting a few yards away with her arms wrapped around her knees, crying and watching him with fearful eyes. She was wearing red sneakers, jeans, and a puffy, white coat. She was about eight years old, with shoulder-length dark hair and blue eyes.

"It's alright," Erik said. "I'm not going to hurt you. Is this your mom?"

She glanced briefly to the woman and then back to him, sniffing and giving just the barest shake of her head.

"Was she your friend? Was she helping you?"

The girl nodded. "Rachel," she whispered after a second or two.

"What's your name?"

"April," she said in a small voice.

"April," he repeated and smiled at her. He glanced at the dead man lying between him and April.

"Did you know that man?"

She shook her head again. Erik let out a small sigh of relief.

"He's not going to hurt you anymore, April. He won't hurt anyone ever again." He glanced down at the woman and thought about what to say. When he looked back up, he saw that the girl was on her feet, taking a few tentative steps towards him. She stopped when she saw him looking at her.

"April," he said. "Do you want to say goodbye to Rachel?"

She seemed unsure at first of what he was asking. But after a few seconds, she walked haltingly over to the dead woman and knelt beside her, crying quietly over her friend.

Erik stayed where he was, giving her all the time she needed. After a couple of minutes, she raised her head and wiped at her eyes, sniffing back tears. She turned to Erik and gave him a sad, lost look.

"Come here," he said quietly. He held his arms out and April came into them, putting her arms around his neck and her head over his shoulder. Erik closed his eyes and hugged her. "It's going to be alright," he whispered. "No one's going to hurt you anymore."

He felt something cold and wet hit his face. When he opened his eyes, he saw it was beginning to snow – big, white flakes falling silently from the blue-gray sky.

"Do you live around here?" Erik asked.

He felt April shake her head.

"Do you know where your home is? Is there someone there to take care of you?"

Another shake.

"I know where we can go. It's a big house with a lot of rooms, maybe more than you can count. We can stay there for as long as we want."

April raised her head off his shoulder.

"Is that where you live?"

He smiled. "I did, for a little while, but I had to leave. I had to keep a promise and say goodbye to someone. I think I'm ready to go back now."

"Does anyone else live there?"

"Yes," he said, remembering the faces of Saundra, Ortiz, McClain, and Ashley. "I think you'll like them."

"Okay," she said and laid her head on his shoulder again.

Erik stood, lifting her in his arms. As the snow continued to fall, he turned and started back to the road that would lead them north, back to Minnesota and the mansion in Elk River.

He didn't know if that was where he belonged now, but he knew it was where he wanted to be.

Printed in Great Britain
by Amazon

26109047R00094